FATAL MISTAKE

FATAL MISTAKE

•

Evalyn Fulmer

AVALON BOOKS

NEW YORK

Published by Avalon Books, an imprint of
Thomas Bouregy & Co., Inc.
160 Madison Avenue, New York, NY 10016

Library of Congress Cataloging-in-Publication Data

Fulmer, Evalyn.
    Fatal mistake / Evalyn Fulmer.
        p. cm.
    ISBN 978-0-8034-7789-6
    1.   Military spouses—Fiction.   2.   Families of military
personnel—Fiction.   3.   Missing persons—Fiction.
4.   Tracking and trailing—Fiction.   I.   Title.
    PS3606.U57F38 2010
    813'.6—dc22
                                                            2010016290

PRINTED IN THE UNITED STATES OF AMERICA
ON ACID-FREE PAPER
BY HADDON CRAFTSMEN, BLOOMSBURG, PENNSYLVANIA

For *my* Marine.

Chapter One

The day dawned gray and silent; the fog rolled in and drifted slowly before swirling around street lamps and tires and sliding through monkey bars and swings and around the lowered ends of seesaws. Very few cars moved in the night, their headlights attempting to penetrate the fog but rebounding back in ghostly silence. The olive-drab jeep moved along the road rapidly but jerked to a stop at the curb. The headlights dimmed, but the occupants made no attempt to climb out of the vehicle. Mendoza, the older of the two men, glanced toward the house just as a sliver of light appeared through a window. The light appeared briefly, then disappeared, and Mendoza settled into the seat. Waiting was part of the job.

Inside the house, the drape had fallen into place. "They're here." Susan looked toward her husband. He was prepared; his gear was already stashed by the door.

"Let's call a truce," he told her. "And we'll talk when I get back."

Susan watched him. She knew what he wanted from her. He wanted an easy leave-taking, an easy good-bye. "You'd better go," she said. He came close and kissed her, but it was a kiss that neither of them enjoyed. Too many angry words had been hurled between them. The room echoed with the heat of their argument, an argument that had taken up most of the night.

Susan watched him as he left, his back straight and his body lean in his utilities. Before he climbed into the jeep, he turned

1

back. Neither of them waved as the jeep pulled away from the curb. They hadn't the heart. Besides, what good could a wave do? What could a wave convey that their words hadn't? When the jeep reached the corner, it turned and disappeared from sight. Susan closed the door and locked it but not before the emptiness moved in. She walked up the stairs to the room she and Kevin shared, the master bedroom. How could it be the "master" bedroom when the master was so seldom there?

The room was beautifully decorated and neat to the point of perfection—even beyond that, to military preciseness—but what did it say about them, about their lives? What story did it tell about the empty hours and the waiting? The room could not even reflect the good times. It provided a passive backdrop to the events of their lives and nothing more.

Susan crossed the room and stared into the mirror. She resembled a Sunday-school teacher in the blue flowered dress with the demure neckline. *Ever the good officer's wife,* she thought. Irritated, she yanked at the dress and popped one of the buttons off, sending it flying across the floor. In her slip she looked less demure, less the proper officer's wife. The slip had been expensive, and it was sensuous, one of Victoria's Secrets, covered with lace—one of the peace offerings Kevin had bought after one of his scheduled missions. He had returned late in the evening, taken a shower, and then reached for her as she turned out lights in the house. His arms had enclosed her, the slip dangled in front of her. He had whispered, "Do you like it?" into her ear, but she had been distracted by his closeness. He'd always had a breathless effect on her, from the first moment she saw him, and now even more so. It was the one area of their marriage he never neglected.

Susan lay down on the bed and waited for sleep to overcome her. Instead of drowsiness, scenes flashed through her mind, less pleasant memories of the night spent in argument. The catalyst had been Kevin's early return from work that day. She'd learned long ago that it was never good news when he came home early. He had walked in bringing gifts, one for her and one each for the children—a toy truck for Bryan and a fat gray stuffed elephant for the baby. Then, with a small flourish, he'd produced a bottle of her favorite perfume. *Guilt gifts.* She'd looked at him, waiting. He'd avoided her eyes, and that's when she knew.

Kevin had moved closer and given her a long and passionate kiss, leaving her breathless in spite of her suspicions.

"Let's go upstairs," he told her, his voice lowered.

Susan backed away. "Bill and Janice are coming over."

"Cancel it," he urged, and he kissed her again.

She looked at him. "Do you have something to tell me?"

"It can wait." He pulled her closer and slid his fingers through her hair. He loved her hair. He cupped the back of her neck with one hand.

She backed away again, fractionally. "Tell me now."

"I don't want to go into it now," he whispered to her, and he looked at her with his smoky eyes, his clean-shaven chin jutting slightly with his resolve.

Susan pulled away and looked at him. She asked, "You're leaving again, right?" It was a fair guess. He had been gone two of the four months they had been at Lejeune. Kevin frowned; he knew what was coming. "Am I right?" she asked.

He looked her in the eyes and sighed. "Yes."

"For how long?"

He hedged. "Not long."

"How long?" she persisted.

"I don't know."

At this pronouncement, Susan flinched. Those were the worst ones. The missions that came up suddenly and had no estimated time of return were the ones she dreaded most. She had gotten it into her head early on that those were also the most dangerous. She walked to the window and looked out. The row of houses visible from her window all looked alike. The only differences were the cars that pulled into the driveways each night and the faces passing through the doors. Kevin came up behind her and put his arms around her. "Don't be upset. I don't think this one will be long." He kissed the back of her neck, trying his best to distract her and to deflect the anger that he knew was coming.

"Where are you going?" She avoided his touch because the proximity of his body created an effect she found difficult to resist. He was lean and hard, the result of continual physical training. Sometimes just being close to him made her breathless and unable to think. And she wanted to think clearly.

"I can't tell you."

She pulled away from him, but she turned finally and faced him. "Why do you have to go? It can't possibly be your turn. You went a few weeks ago. Can't they send someone else this time?"

His eyes flicked away from hers, and he mumbled something about it having just come up, but he added, "It's not a game, Susan. We don't sit around and discuss who went last and who wants to go."

But she felt it *was* a game to them, in part at least. And it was one they enjoyed. He looked guilty, and it hit her then. "You want to go, don't you? Don't you?"

His body, his shoulders, fell just a little, and he sighed. "Yes," he admitted. "I want to take this mission. It's—"

"You volunteered for it?" Her voice increased in volume while his remained unchanged.

"Yes." He had finally said it, finally admitted it.

Her eyes, those large, luminous eyes that he'd loved from the first moment he'd seen them, stared at him, hurt, angry. "Susan—"

"Do you like leaving us? Do you *want* to spend so much time away from the children? And from me?"

"Of course not." He reached for her—or tried to—but she managed to elude his grasp. "You know I want to be with you, but I have to do my job. You knew about all this when you married me."

There was that. There was always that. And it was true

enough. She had known from the start what their life would be like. She might not have been familiar enough with the military to form an accurate picture, but she'd known it would involve absences.

A hungry baby had ended the argument at that point but only for a short time.

Susan lay alone now on the bed, remembering yet not wanting to remember, until the anger finally abated and she grew sleepy. The sound of crying jolted her from her drowsiness, and she went into the next room, where Chrissy lay clutching the bed rails. Susan picked her up and carried her back to her own room to change and feed her. She put the baby to her breast and watched her suck hungrily. Such perfection in the little fingers and the toes and the mouth—it never ceased to amaze her. Once the hunger pangs were gone, the baby was content, and she smiled up at her mother happily.

How simple it was to fill an infant's needs, how easy for a baby to be content. Not so with adults. Susan thought for a few minutes and then put Chrissy in the middle of the big bed. Then, without premeditation or any conscious thought of having come to a decision, she pulled on a pair of jeans and a shirt and opened the closet door. The top shelf was piled with suitcases, the matching set her parents had given her for her graduation. She pulled them down and began to fill them.

Chapter Two

The drone of engines, all the silent looks and sober glances exchanged between the two rows of seats facing each other—Kevin Brannigan contemplated them as his head pounded. His mind raced backward even as the plane moved ahead. The entire mood of the mission had been somber, almost gloomy. There'd been none of the lighter, time-passing banter among the men that was so common in these situations. Brannigan wondered if the fault was his. He had spoken very little since leaving the Azores or, for that matter, stateside.

His mind was crammed full of the bitter argument he'd had with Susan. He could think of nothing else. Why was it always necessary for the two of them to have a major blowup every time he had an assignment? It was his job, and it was what he wanted to do. He had never really considered anything else. As early as he could remember, he had wanted to be a Marine. How much of that was due to his father's being a career officer, he didn't know; he just knew it was the only thing he had ever wanted to do. He felt charged when he was engaged on recon missions. Why couldn't Susan understand that? None of it had bothered her in the beginning; what had happened to change that? The thing that worried him most was the intensity of their latest argument. It had flared hotter than any they'd had before and would have lasted longer if he hadn't cut it off by walking out the door. Once Susan figured out that he had volunteered for the new assignment, she

6

had accused him of a lack of interest in their lives, even neglect. How could she think that? When he was with them, it was great. The two kids had added more to their lives than he had thought possible, even if it grew chaotic at times. And Susan? There had never been anyone like her in his life before.

Susan had a face to grace magazine covers, and it had, in fact, during the two years she had modeled. She wore her hair long, well past her shoulders, and it curled softly around her upper arms and back. The sunlight always caught it and turned it lighter than it already was. Her eyes revealed depths that pulled him in till he thought he could happily drown in them. That had never changed.

Susan didn't have the height for major success in the modeling business. When she realized it, her independent streak reared its head. She didn't want to follow paths uselessly or be told what she could or couldn't do. Her independent spirit had always been evident. If she had any flaw, it was her unexpected twists of sudden insecurity that gave her a vulnerability that made him want to take care of her. That vulnerability overwhelmed him and was very appealing, but he worried that she was too trusting, of anyone and everyone.

Her career had been cut short. Was that it? Did she miss the excitement and challenge of the working world, the lure of earning her own money? Their last argument had evolved from the time-consuming nature of his career to the empty hours she continually faced while he was gone. They'd argued before over the possibility of filling those hours with work of some kind, but there they always hit a snag. He remained adamant on one point: he would not have his children farmed out to day care. And Susan didn't want that either, so what was the solution?

Mendoza slid into the space beside Brannigan, interrupting his thoughts. "The men are a little uptight," he said.

"Why?" Brannigan asked. "This mission's no worse than others they've been on."

"It's the tension in the air . . . more than usual, and they sense it."

Brannigan looked at Mendoza long and hard. He knew what his friend was implying. He and Mendoza had seen a lot of action together, in Kuwait and Panama. Now Brannigan leaned his head back and said, "The tension may be due to other things. It may have nothing to do with the mission itself."

Mendoza opened his mouth to speak but closed it, saying nothing.

"Too much time to think," Brannigan muttered. "That's the problem."

"Yeah," Mendoza agreed. "It can work on you."

Mendoza was an inch or two shorter than Brannigan, and his hair was a true black. In addition his eyes were so dark, it was impossible to see the delineating line between the iris and the pupil except in direct sunlight. He was a friendly guy and got along with everyone, often hosting football parties with his big-screen TV and laughing and joking with everyone, but he could be serious too, and Brannigan appreciated that side of him most when they worked together.

They sat in silence for a while, absorbed in their own individual thoughts, until Brannigan asked, "Have you ever had trouble with your wife about these missions?"

"Trouble with my old lady? Me?" Mendoza grinned. His grin was infectious and almost always soon reached everyone around him. "Nah," he added, "we don't have any trouble. She's always real glad to see me when I get home."

"Does she object to your leaving all the time?"

"Oh, she doesn't like it, but she doesn't say much. I let her know how important she is to me every time I get back." He grinned again. "Women don't like being second best. They don't want to think you love anything more than you love them. Not even the Corps."

"Is that it?" Brannigan asked. *Could it be that simple?*

"Well, my wife might be different, but I don't think so.

Women are women. Our kind of work can put a real strain on relationships. Some more than others."

"Would you change what you do for the sake of your marriage?"

"Not me. I found what I like best. There are a lot of poor slobs out there who don't know what they want, but I know. And I'm doing it." Brannigan nodded; he understood the sentiment. "Besides, it shouldn't have to come to that. Take some time when you get back and let Susan know how special she is. Take her out and spend time with her without the kids. It doesn't have to be anything fancy, just some time where it's just you and her and she knows that all you're thinking about is her." Mendoza grinned again.

Brannigan smiled. "You may be on to something. You may be right."

"'Course I'm right. You know what I did with my old lady one time after I was gone for two months?"

Brannigan looked skeptical. "Do I want to know?"

Mendoza laughed. "Sure. I took her on a picnic and then to the zoo. We had more fun than we'd had in a long time, even though it was nothing special. We even rode the elephants. There we were with two dozen school kids in line behind us, and we took our turn on the elephants. It was like we were high-school kids again." Mendoza leaned his head back and closed his eyes, lost in thought. "Maybe we should do that again."

Brannigan turned to look out the small window nearby at the diaphanous quality of the clouds. Why did it never seem that easy? The disappointment in Susan's eyes had made it more difficult to face her each time he had a mission. But he could make sure they got away for some time together when he returned, maybe to those cabins he had heard about near the beach. Just the two of them.

Forty miles to Atlanta, and it was obvious it had all been a mistake. Especially the idea of traveling by car. Six o'clock in the evening, and the three of them were exhausted. The baby cried, Bryan whined alternately for cookies and his toys, and Susan's back ached from sitting in the same position for so long. She tried to interest the baby in a bottle of juice, and she talked to Bryan about the fun he would have with his cousin. Anything to distract him.

The journey had begun well enough. When Susan carried the bags out to the garage, she had hesitated, looking from the small SUV she always drove to the sports car that was Kevin's. It would serve him right if she took his car and left him the SUV. His was the newer of the two, but the extra space in hers became the deciding factor.

When it came to writing a note to Kevin, she was at a loss. What could she say? That she couldn't take it anymore? That she might as well be living alone? After deliberating for an hour, she had decided to call him when he returned. Maybe she could explain it to him then.

The call to her sister was more difficult because she could not put it off. Sharon was surprised to hear from her and launched into a colorful account of family news before Susan gathered the courage to explain why she had called. Sharon was speechless, and that had never happened before, but when she collected herself, she urged Susan to come for as long as she wanted. When Sharon learned that Susan intended to drive, she protested noisily, but Susan had insisted it was just what she needed. The long drive would give her plenty of time to think. And it had seemed like a good idea at the time.

Now she was not so certain. The rush-hour traffic of Atlanta occupied her thoughts for the next half hour until she was so exasperated that she wanted to scream. A sign caught her eye, and she pulled into an Exxon station, grateful for the credit card she'd remembered to bring along.

Another credit card bought a room for the night and an evening meal ordered from room service. She had no energy left to take the children out to a restaurant, and she had absolutely no desire to be out in public with two overtired and grumpy children.

The meal and a warm bath lulled the two children into slumber, but she lay in the unfamiliar room with the lights out and thought of Kevin. What was he doing at that exact moment? And an even bigger question, where *was* he at that moment? The argument between them and the day's activities since had drained her emotionally as well as physically. She wanted nothing more than a good night's sleep, but even with her eyes closed, she thought of Kevin.

Chapter Three

The night air dried the sweat on their faces and felt good only by comparison with the stale air of the cramped quarters belowdecks. Brannigan moved across the deck toward the small group of men mustered together. The rubber dinghies were ready; the men had blackened their faces. Brayhill and Williams loaded the night-vision lenses onto the cameras and put them on board the Kodiaks. Blake had the NODs, the night optical devices that he passed to each member of the reconnaissance unit. The Kodiaks were lowered, and the squad followed them over the side.

Brannigan had briefed the men on the nature of their mission. Rumors abounded before any mission and led to guesses about destination and the reasons for the recon. Atmospheric conditions had prevented clear satellite pictures of the coastline, but a flurry of intercepted e-mails had murmured that another buildup of troops and equipment had begun in areas suspected of containing stockpiles of weapons of mass destruction. The mission was simple: they were to go in, reconnoiter the area, take as many photographs as possible, then get out without engaging the enemy. The atmosphere between the U.S. and the country in question never settled for long and remained unstable.

The water of the Persian Gulf appeared calm as they dropped into the kayaks. Mendoza called for noise discipline, and silence fell over the unit like a wool blanket. The dinghies moved off and aimed straight toward the coast, their motors making little noise. As land became visible, the engines were turned off, and the dinghies pitched with the movements of the sea. As the men picked up oars to cover the remaining distance, they worked silently, thrusting each paddle with fast, even strokes into the water and back.

The surf broke against the shoreline as they pulled the boats up and onto the land and stashed them. The men's equipment had been sealed in waterproof packs, and all of it was carried on their backs. In silence the men pulled out the NODs and strapped them on. The landscape immediately took on the eerie glow cast by the infrared lenses. Nothing appeared on the scene in any direction. No movement visible at all. At a sign from Kevin Brannigan, the unit separated into two squads and moved off into the night.

Brannigan's squad consisted of Brayhill, Hutton, Williams, Rodriguez, and Brooks. The six of them climbed the coastline and headed inland for two miles. The first sign they'd reached their destination was the fence, eight feet high, wired on top, and guarded. They waited until the patrol passed on. Hutton clipped the fence, and the men slipped into the compound. The size of the barracks and the number of tanks and antiaircraft weapons solidified the suspicion that large numbers of troops and equipment were being massed. Something was up. Brayhill snapped digital pictures as they continued through the black night. The tension was palpable; the men remained alert. The sight of thirty F150s, fifteen to twenty mobile surface-to-air missile launchers, and an equal number of surface-to-surface missiles were enough to confirm all suspicions.

The squad crossed the compound and slid back through the fence without incident. Security was lax, the patrol now nowhere to be seen. The compound had been devoid of activity until they moved twenty-five feet past the fence in the direction they'd come from, and then they encountered human activity. Three men walking. Brayhill and Hutton knocked two of them out, wrestled the third down with a knife to his throat, then realized belatedly that the men were not soldiers or guards. By all appearances they were villagers out for some pre-dawn fishing. Hutton struck the third man hard enough to give him something to tell his grandchildren. The man slid to his knees and then collapsed onto the ground. The squad picked up the pace and moved double-time back to the shore.

The dinghies were retrieved, and the men waited, but there was no sign of Mendoza's squad. Brannigan paced, debating on a course of action. He stopped to consult his watch at 0300 hours.

Brayhill asked, "Want me to take a look-see, Captain?"

"No," Brannigan told him. "We'll give them another five minutes."

Suddenly shots rang out, followed by the sound of running feet, and all of it heading toward them.

"Into the Kodiaks," Brannigan yelled, "and start moving out!"

"But, Cap'n . . ."

"Get going!" Brannigan shouted.

Mendoza's men scrambled toward the shore, pulled the boats into the water, and moved out. Mendoza, the last to appear, had been wounded. His men pulled him into the Kodiak. Shots flew over their heads, and Brannigan yelled, "What happened?"

"We engaged the enemy, sir."

Mendoza's wound was in the upper arm, but he reassured them that it was nothing. Brannigan suspected it was a matter of pride or the silent code they all lived by. A wound was a badge of honor, and Mendoza would not admit to pain. By the time dawn arrived, Mendoza's wound had been treated, and the men were sacked out safely on the ship as it plowed steadily through the sea.

Abilene in the sweltering sunshine. How come the country singers never sang about that? Susan turned the air conditioner one notch higher, but it failed to respond with cooler air. *Great.*

This would be a dandy time for the Freon to run out. She pulled fruit and cookies from her bag for Bryan, who complained that he was hungry. Why hadn't she thought to bring an ice chest with her? But she knew the answer to that. The truth of the matter was that she'd left in anger, and she was a terrible traveler under the best of circumstances. She'd been that way since she was a child. The open countryside was beautiful, but she wanted to see it all, and right now. On the few trips her family had taken when she was young, she'd driven them all crazy by wanting to stop and see every town, every marker, and every thing.

Why hadn't she resisted the impulse to drive? She could have been in Phoenix by now, sipping a cold drink and pouring her heart out to her sister. Except Sharon wasn't someone you poured your heart out to. Oh, she listened. She listened patiently, but then she'd have a twelve-point plan for you to implement in your life immediately in order to solve your problems.

Susan looked at the children: Bryan had fallen asleep with cookie scattered across his face and clothes and half the car seat, and the baby cried loudly. Susan tried her best to cajole her into a better mood. Nothing worked, but eventually Chrissy gave up and fell asleep too.

For a full thirty minutes only the sound of the air conditioner droned in her ears. No music. In fact, as further testament to the ill-planned trip, she'd left her music CDs in the house, and when she'd discovered it, she couldn't believe it. Music was a necessity, like food and water, to Susan. And music helped with the children sometimes. The radio saved her, especially in and around the urban areas, but eventually the signals grew weak, and it wasn't worth the effort of fiddling with the buttons.

While the children slept, she could cover more miles—fewer distractions. That's what she hoped for now, but of course it didn't work. Both of the children woke in a short time and were twice as cranky as before. They began to sound like a disgruntled chorus, but since the windows were up all, the people in passing cars were unaware of the pandemonium inside unless they caught a quick glance at the open mouths and red, tearful faces.

No amount of pleading or promises worked on either one of them. Finally she could take it no longer. The next town of any size was Big Spring, and the minute they reached it, Susan pulled into the first decent motel she saw. The tears stopped long enough for the three of them to stand in front of the desk to sign the register, but as soon as they got into the room, the crying began again, in unison. Susan felt an almost uncontrollable urge to join in, but she resisted long enough to give them each a quick bath, an equally quick dinner, and a very early bedtime.

In the morning she would take the time to buy an ice chest and some healthy snacks and bottled water to fill it. She should have done it sooner. The trip had gone well as far as Atlanta, but at that point everything had begun to fall apart. The exciting promise of his cousin's house had worn off for Bryan. At his age, he just wanted to be there. The anger that had motivated Susan to begin the journey had begun to wear thin when she was confronted with the realities of getting the three of them across three-fourths of the country. Susan resisted the desire to turn around and go home because she had already passed the point where it would be easier to go on than return. Or thought she had.

What sounded really, really good to her was a long soak in a warm bath. If she'd brought lavender oil and candles, she would have stayed in the tub until the water grew cold. In the air-conditioned motel, the warm water felt good. Her muscles had cramped from sitting so long in the same position. The tension hadn't helped either. The children's crying had been one thing, but added to that, somewhere in a part of her mind, her thoughts remained on Kevin and the miserable way they'd left things between them.

When she climbed out of the bath, she toweled off and

dressed in the white silk pajamas that were her favorites because they were so comfortable. She rubbed her hands along
her sleeves, the fabric cool and smooth to the touch. Where
was Kevin now, she wondered.

Chapter Four

The land around Midland and Odessa stretched out flat for miles, hot and dusty miles. Oil wells cluttered the landscape; some no longer pumped the black ooze that had put this part of Texas onto the map. Susan drove on, and what seemed like many hot miles later a town appeared in a shimmer of heat. She drove across the bridge and into the town of Pecos, Texas, searching for a gas station. One mile down the road she found an Exxon station that offered full service. God bless the anachronisms of small-town America. She'd been saved the ordeal of getting out and pumping her own gas while struggling to keep two kids happy in the car. A tall, teenage kid sauntered out of the air-conditioned office toward the pumps. Skinny and with a headful of unruly, carrot-colored hair, he appeared incapable of hurrying. His jeans and work shirt were well worn, the pant legs a little high-water on him. Susan slid the windows down, and the West Texas heat and wind blew into the car, bringing with it the smell of dust and stale oil. Bryan was delighted to have the windows open; he unbuckled his seat belt, scrambled to the window, poked his head out as far as he could, and said, "Hi!"

"Hi yourself." On closer inspection the teenager looked as if someone had spray-painted his face with light brown dots.

"Mommy forgetted to get gas," Bryan volunteered.

"Oh, yeah? What's your name?" The teen set the pump

handle to dispense automatically and pulled a squeegee from a bucket and started washing the windshield.

"My name is Bwyan." He held up three fingers. "I'm this many."

"Is that right? An older guy, huh?"

"The baby's name is Kwissy. She has a tooth."

"Only one? It must be hard for her to eat apples."

Bryan giggled. "She doesn't eat apples."

The windshield cleared of bug bodies, the teen turned his attention back to the pump. When it clicked, he pulled the nozzle out and replaced it on the pump. Then he ruffled Brian's hair, took the Exxon card Susan gave him, and went into the office to run the charge.

Bryan jumped on the backseat, obviously enjoying his freedom, but Susan sat miserably in the front. The heat seemed to suck the oxygen from the air. Perspiration trickled down her back as she waited. The gawky teen returned with her credit card and receipt. Soon she pulled out onto the open road. She faced the glare of the sun and the pavement ahead with its narrow stripe that went on forever. The scenery around her had lost any appeal; she just wanted the trip to end. She didn't regret the impulse to take the trip; she just wished she had made the decision to fly.

The car ran smoothly, and, for a while, so did the children. Susan pulled a jar of bananas out of her bag and tried to feed the baby as she drove, but when she moved over the center stripe twice, she realized what she was doing was crazy. She pulled into the first rest stop, fed a snack to both of the children, and then headed back onto the highway again.

I-20 ended abruptly at I-30 close to the foot of the Davis Mountains, and it was there that Susan turned into a more direct westerly direction, drove through a small town called Kent, and continued on, already tired. More highway, always more highway. The air conditioner was cranked to its peak, but the heat oozing through the glass never eased. What had it been like crossing this country in a covered wagon or on horseback? And what compensation would there be at the end of each day other than the absence of the sun's glare and the chance to have your feet on the ground? Susan gained a new level of respect for the pioneers and early settlers of the West. One thing that might have made their journey better than hers would have been the absence of billboards and signs and the litter of a vast and growing nation. The land would have been endlessly clear, revealing its own stark beauty. Would that have made their travails worthwhile? No, but she supposed that the promise of new homes, free land, and open spaces was what drove the early settlers.

A red light flashed on the instrument panel, and Susan slowed to see what was wrong. The temperature gauge. Her stomach sank; the trip hadn't been difficult enough? Maybe the car needed oil? Susan stopped the car and climbed out. She struggled to get the hood up. With that accomplished, she stared at the engine. It was overheating—that much was certain—but why? The radiator cap was too hot to touch. She had to wait for it to cool.

Fifteen minutes later, the heat in the car had become more intense than the heat outside. They couldn't bear it much longer. Her shirt clung to her back like another layer of skin; perspiration ran down her temples and the backs of her knees. Another five minutes and she knew she had to do something. She grabbed a bottle of water she'd bought earlier and, using a disposable diaper, she twisted the radiator cap open and poured half the water into it. She hesitated to use all of their water.

The car started immediately and instilled new hope; she pulled out onto the highway and soon saw a sign that read twenty-seven miles to Van Horn ahead and three miles to Fleming down the road to the right. She hesitated briefly but pulled off the highway to the right onto a narrow road that led to Fleming. And that, as it turned out, was the biggest mistake she'd made since leaving Camp Lejeune. One mile down the road the car died, and steam whooshed out from under the hood in a large vaporous mass. *Terrific,* she thought. She pulled the map out. According to the map, the road she was on led to the Apache Mountains and boasted nothing else but the small town of Fleming. Would anyone even come down this isolated road before dark? *Oh, no, dark. Night.* Now, that was something she hadn't considered. Being stranded out here in the dark. That was not a prospect she would relish. She looked off the road at the land around her. What might crawl out from under the brush in the dark? Belatedly she realized what a mistake it had been to leave the main highway. She faced the option of either walking to the town of Fleming, a couple of miles away, or she could walk the mile back to the highway and flag someone down. Neither sounded easy or appealing in this heat. She wondered if the town of Fleming would even have a garage.

She pulled her cell phone out of her bag but stopped and thought. Who would she call? She didn't know anyone out here. One look at the display on the phone, and she realized it didn't matter. She hadn't charged it. The phone was dead.

Susan took a small drink of the remaining water, feeling the cool liquid trickle down her dry throat. She cooled the children off by wiping their faces with baby wipes. They were so beautiful. She sometimes stopped in the middle of doing some small act for them, like now, and marveled at how wonderful they were. Had she placed them in jeopardy by bringing them on this journey? She shook herself mentally. The car needed a repair—that was all. After that they would be back on their way to Arizona, to her sister's house.

The car doors stood open to let in any available breeze. Bryan pushed at the heavy doors and succeeded in closing one of them. Susan stood beside the car bouncing the baby and watching Bryan work at the doors.

A dust cloud gathered on the horizon behind the car, and Susan watched as it grew. Finally the cloud materialized into a sleek white car that stopped beside her. A Cadillac, of all things. How surreal. The door on the driver's side opened, and a tall, silver-haired man in a white Stetson stepped out. He looked across the wide hood at them. Bryan stopped his playing and stared at the man in the white hat, speechless. The baby had even stopped crying.

He was big man, more than six feet and husky. Middle-aged and striking in appearance, he circled the front of his car, and Susan saw that he wore gray boots and gray pants with the largest silver belt buckle she had ever seen outside of a rodeo.

The exterior of his car was spotlessly white, and the sunlight reflected off the shiny metal trim. The shine was enough to cause spots before her eyes. Even the interior of the car was white. Added to that, the man's hair was white, as was his Stetson and the starched shirt he wore. In the middle of all that was the startling blue of his eyes. All of it created a picture that made it difficult for Susan not to stare. He looked like someone who'd stepped out of a movie or a book, larger than life.

"Need some help?" he asked. When she didn't respond, he said, "Ma'am?"

"Uh . . . yes. My car overheated. It won't go any farther."

He looked her over carefully, which was not the reaction she'd expected. The appraisal was frank and openly admiring. He appeared lost in thought, but then he focused and told her, "You aren't anything like what I'm used to finding along this road."

Susan laughed. She was seated on the outer edge of the car seat and facing out the door. She caught a glimpse of herself in the rearview mirror—damp hair clinging to her forehead, perspiration running down her neck. Maybe both of them had been out in the sun too long.

"I'm John Cressman." He had to visibly pull his gaze from her face. "Who is this?"

Susan turned toward Bryan and laughed. He stared at the man as if he'd seen a ghost or an angel. And maybe the man *was* an angel of sorts. She knew he was about to rescue them. "This is Bryan, and I'm Susan Brannigan."

"Susan." He repeated her name as if he liked the sound of it. "Let me take a look at your car, Susan."

He bent over the engine, checking hoses, water level, and the radiator itself. Pulling a white handkerchief from his back pocket, he wiped his hands. "I'm afraid you've got a real problem. The radiator's blown a hole. Most likely the whole thing will have to be replaced."

"Oh, no." Susan pushed damp hair back from her face. What should she do? She'd like to scrap the car and take a plane for the remainder of the trip, but she couldn't just leave it. And where might the nearest airport be? "Are you sure?" she asked. "Is there any way to fix it temporarily?"

He looked doubtful. "I don't think so."

Bryan had climbed in and out of the car several times, and he suddenly fell out onto the gravel at the edge of the road and shrieked. Susan picked him up and dusted him off. His knees were skinned, one was bleeding, and tears slid down his cheeks. He saw the blood and cried harder, big crocodile tears that dropped onto his cheeks. The baby, seeing Bryan crying, began to cry, and her face, which had already been red from the heat, turned a brighter red.

John Cressman assessed the situation and took action. He slammed the hood shut, picked Bryan up, sat him on the car seat, then pulled a first-aid kit from his car. With surprising gentleness he scraped the dirt and gravel from Bryan's knees and then wiped them with an antiseptic. And then, much to Bryan's delight, he placed a large Band-Aid on each knee.

"I think you've made a friend for life," Susan told him. "A Band-Aid on any injury, new or old, is one of his favorite things."

Cressman patted Bryan's shoulder and turned toward Susan. "Look," he said, "clearly you need help. Your car's not going anywhere in the condition it's in. Let's put your things into my car, and I'll run you into town to the garage. We'll get Ed to pick your car up and take a look at it. He's a good friend, so I can get him to come out here right away."

Susan thought about it. She didn't know this man, but what else could she do? The children had to get out of the heat. For that matter, she needed to get out of the heat too. There was no choice but to accept his kind offer of help.

Cressman pulled their luggage from the rear while she gathered the loose paraphernalia from inside the car. He stashed everything in the trunk of his car, then closed her SUV, locked it, and gave her the keys. Susan smiled. The place didn't exactly look like a high-crime area. Would anyone even come down this road, and if so, would they have any interest in her SUV?

The blast of cooled air began to revive her spirits, while both of the children stared at the man and the all-white interior of the Cadillac. They stopped their fussing, but they held on to their mother with a tight grip.

"Where are you from?" Cressman asked suddenly. In the light of her car trouble and his rescue, the question hit her as incongruous, but when she thought about it and relaxed into the white leather seat, she realized that people traveling always asked that question.

"I'm from Oregon originally, but we live in North Carolina now. We're driving out to Phoenix to visit my sister."

"You're driving all that distance with two small children and no one else to help you?"

"I know—I should have flown. Believe me, *that* became obvious by the second day, and I never even thought I'd have this kind of trouble."

"You never know with cars. They're fine one day, and the next day you find you've got a passel of trouble."

"I believe you, especially now. Do you live near here?"

"I have a place out past Fleming. I was just on my way back from doing some business in Midland."

What kind of business did one do in Midland? "Well, it's fortunate for us that you got there when you did. Another thirty minutes and we would have baked out there."

Cressman looked out at the sun-brightened landscape. "It is

a hot one today," he said. "No place for little guys like you," he told Bryan. "Not along the road stuck in a hot car anyway." Bryan merely stared and remained where he was, clutching his mother's shirt.

The town appeared on the horizon, and Susan looked forward to finding a place for the children to rest while the repair work was done on her car. The town couldn't be totally insignificant if it produced cowboys in Cadillacs. When she saw it up close, she had to revise her opinion. A group of buildings huddled together in the sun-baked landscape, a post office and grocery store dominating the scene, obviously reflecting the hub of life in the community. There was a café tucked between the gas station and a place called Lyla's Boutique. A sign in the window of the boutique advertised DVDs and videos to rent. Behind the boutique the Sea Ranch Inn stretched in an *L* shape. The *Sea*? The Dairy Queen rounded out what the town had to offer. And, who knew? An evening at the Dairy Queen might be the high point of the week in the town of Fleming.

Cressman pulled into the drive of the gas station and got out, leaving the motor running and the cold air blowing. He went through the garage doors in search of his friend. He came back with a middle-aged man in greasy overalls with a thick head of hair and brown eyes that crinkled in a friendly-looking way at the corners.

"Susan, this is Ed. He's going to check out your car and bring it back here. If he can't fix it, no one can."

Ed laughed. "If you'll give me the keys, ma'am, I'll pick it up and bring it in. I should know something in an hour or two."

Susan gave him the keys and thanked him. She promised to come back later. Cressman climbed back into the car. "Now, how about letting me buy dinner for you while you're waiting?"

Susan hesitated. "I've been thinking. It's getting late, and the car may take a few hours. I should get a room for the night."

"That's a good idea. I'll take you to the motel so you can settle in, then I'll pick you up in half an hour for dinner."

Susan hadn't agreed to have dinner with him, and the truth was, she really wanted a bath and a nap. She hesitated, trying to think how to get out of it. A sandwich and soup in bed in front of the TV sounded good right about now.

Cressman smiled. "Come on, you need to eat. Let me treat you."

Susan looked at him. She didn't even know him, but he'd been kind to help them, and it was true, she had to eat. And, more important, the children needed to eat.

"Make it an hour. We'll need time to get cleaned up."

Chapter Five

The delay grated on Brannigan's nerves because there was no reason for it. Mendoza had been treated on board the ship and released for the flight home. The hang-up occurred when they reached the Azores. Transport assignments bogged down with the continual flux of troops in and out of the region. Brannigan had to create a little flack of his own to obtain results. He went from a pimply faced corporal sitting behind a desk to a master Sergeant ten years his senior to a second lieutenant who, typically, had no idea which end was up. A full day was lost with nothing left to do but sit in temporary quarters and stare at the walls. It was the single most irritating hunk of crap in the military—*hurry up and wait.*

Now that the mission was over, Brannigan's tension increased in direct proportion to the anticipation of the time when he would be faced with untangling the emotional mess he'd left behind. *Calm down,* he told himself. *We've argued before. It will all straighten out once we're together again.* The thing of it was, he needed to speak to Susan. Now that the mission was complete and he could focus on his personal life, he felt an unexplainable and urgent need to speak to her. The urgency grew until he felt desperate. *Just to hear her voice.* Yes, that's what he needed, to hear her voice. He would call her. Once he heard her voice, the soft timbre of her voice, he'd feel better. He could ease the indefinable fear and calm down.

Thirty minutes later he had tried twice to reach Susan by

phone, but he hadn't succeeded. If anything, he felt worse than before. There had been no answer at the house. Where could she be? Back in the room assigned to him, he took his shirt off and sat on the bed and thought about that last argument. She'd been upset enough when she learned that he had volunteered for the assignment, but when their argument had evolved into the proverbial blast from the past, every remembered misdeed, they'd moved onto dangerous ground. He knew he was sometimes unreasonable, and the thought ate at him. Kevin recognized Susan's need for some outlet of her own, a hobby or committee or volunteer work, but he preferred she not go to work. He earned enough money for the four of them. Susan had made good money as a model before they married, but it wasn't about the money. She would have made a success of her life with or without him, but timing was everything, and he'd always had it. He'd known from the first that she was the one he wanted, and he had moved fast. They were married within six weeks, and Susan had dropped her art classes at UCLA and cancelled her modeling schedule because they'd moved to a new duty station within two months. Was that it? Did she miss all that?

Kevin tried phoning again. Still no answer. What time was it at Lejeune? He didn't know, but he was certain she should be home. He jumped as a knock on the door interrupted his thoughts.

"Who is it?" His voice sounded rude, and he knew it.

"Mendoza."

"Come in." Brannigan couldn't help but wonder what Mendoza wanted. All Brannigan wanted was to be left alone.

Mendoza stuck his head into the doorway. "May I speak to you, sir?"

"Of course." Brannigan stood up.

Mendoza held his right hand behind his back; the other hung in a sling.

"Something came up, and I thought I should bring it to your attention."

"What is it?" Brannigan asked.

Mendoza pulled his arm forward, producing a bottle of Scotch. "Thought you could use some company."

"Yeah, that sounds good." Brannigan pushed his fingers through his hair, leaving it looking like furrows in a newly plowed field. He stepped into the bathroom and came out with two clear plastic cups, and the two of them sat down and turned their attention to the bottle.

Brannigan was struck by a thought that had occurred to him on similar occasions. His father would be speechless if he could see him now. Major General David Brannigan would never sit down with an enlisted man to share a bottle of Scotch. Of course it was possible Kevin didn't know his father as well as he thought. What about Susan? Did he know her well? He thought he did. That depressed him further. He rubbed his eyes with a thumb and forefinger, reached for the Scotch, and poured a quick second drink.

Mendoza looked at him over the rim of his own glass. "Want to talk about it?"

Brannigan stared down into his cup. "No."

"You sure?"

"How's your arm?" Brannigan asked, shifting the conversation to other topics as the level in the bottle lowered perceptibly.

The motel was old. There was no getting around that. It had been built so long ago, each unit had a kitchenette. The bathroom was antiquated but clean, and there was plenty of hot water, which did wonders to restore Susan's mood. A bath and the freedom of being out of the car helped the children's moods as well. Bryan explored every corner of the room while Chrissy picked at the appliquéd flowers on her quilt. When John Cressman arrived to pick them up, Susan felt refreshed, and the three of them were ready.

Everyone in the café knew everyone else, yet no one seemed surprised to see strangers. Susan's best guess was that she had already been the topic of conversation from one end of town to the other from the moment she'd arrived in Cressman's Cadillac. After they settled into a booth, they endured ten minutes of hungry children eating crackers and scattering the crumbs everywhere. When the food arrived, it was so much better than Susan had expected, she had to readjust her first impression of the place. Her appetite had disappeared, banished by the heat, but it returned with the first bite. By the time dessert arrived, the baby had fallen asleep in her carrier seat, and Bryan had pushed his vegetables around until he caught sight of the brownies. Cressman laughed at the look of pure delight on Bryan's face.

"I'd forgotten how much fun children can be," he said.

Susan looked at Bryan and the baby; she hadn't found them particularly fun during the last few days, but, to be fair, she hadn't been much fun either. "Do you have children?"

"I did. A boy. But he died very young." He patted Bryan's arm. "May I ask you a question?" Cressman's blue eyes avoided hers.

"Of course." She could not imagine what it was that he wanted to ask.

"Where's their father?"

Oh. Good question, she thought. Cressman looked into her eyes. Maybe he saw more than she wanted him to see, more than she wanted anyone to see.

"He's in the Marines. I'm on my way to visit my sister in Phoenix."

"I know some people in Phoenix. What's her name?"

"Stillwell—Sharon Stillwell."

"We're going to see Jimmy," Bryan announced.

"Jimmy is his cousin," Susan explained.

"Jimmy is four. He's this many." Bryan held up four fingers.

Cressman smiled. "You're going to have fun playing with your cousin."

"Jimmy has lots of Hot Wheels. He told me." Bryan stuffed half a brownie into his mouth and wiped his sticky fingers across the front of his shirt.

"Oh, so your husband is going to join you in Phoenix?"

"No. Well, I don't know." Susan glanced at Bryan. "Maybe later."

Susan's face revealed too much; Cressman could read her easily. He studied her carefully, her long blond hair curled softly around her shoulders. The expression in her eyes was troubled—he felt sure of it. He watched as she spoke to Bryan, her lips well defined and soft. He knew they were soft because he had watched them so many times before. He had felt them, and he had tasted them. They were Ellen's lips. They moved like Ellen's lips and smiled in the same slow, sensuous curve.

His expression was so intense, it created an awkward silence for a moment, but Susan had a tendency to talk when she felt uncomfortable and to worry about making everyone else comfortable.

Now she asked, "Have you always lived out here?"

"Since I was a boy," he told her. "I lived in Dallas until the age of ten. My father bought the ranch at that time. It's the same place I have now."

"Is it large?"

"We only grow them big out here," he drawled, and then he laughed. "Maybe I could show it to you."

Surprised at this, Susan told him, "I don't think we'll be here long enough."

"Your car may take a while," he warned.

A knot formed in the pit of her stomach. "Then I'll have to rethink my travel plans. There must be a bus that comes by here."

"Not often," he warned. And then he hesitated; he picked up a spoon and turned it over again and again as he turned over what he was thinking in his mind as well. Clearly John Cressman was not a man who talked often or easily, but he wanted to say something, and finally he did. He blurted out, "What's got you so unhappy? Your face, your eyes, even your body language all add up to a very unhappy picture. What is it that's made you so unhappy?"

Surprised, Susan wondered, *Is my face that transparent? Is it really all out there for anyone to see?*

Cressman looked deeper into her eyes and held them in a direct gaze. "I realize you don't know me, but sometimes a stranger offers a better listening ear than a friend. With a stranger you can forget what you told them afterward, and he'll forget it too. Less clutter. Mentally, that is."

"I'm fine," she reassured him as well as herself. "I've been stressed because of the trip. Traveling with children isn't easy. Especially very young ones. And now the car . . ." She laughed, but it sounded hollow and meaningless to her ears. She felt incapable of giving a straightforward, albeit simple, answer.

Susan could not have predicted that before the evening ended, she would be sitting, with Bryan asleep on her lap, telling John Cressman the details of her argument with Kevin and everything that had led up to her decision to leave. By that point he felt like an old friend, but how much of that stemmed from her need to talk, how much from exhaustion, and how much from the glass of wine she drank, she was not altogether certain.

Hadn't she been wanting—seeking, even—a listening ear since the argument with Kevin? Wasn't that the truth behind her sudden desire to drive cross-country to see her sister? And it surely was not happenstance that she had chosen Sharon to visit. She wanted confirmation that she was not at fault, and who better to give that than her own sister? All of this had come to her in a rush without being reasoned out. She hadn't sat and thought about where to go, whom to go to—it had just come to her. Sharon would listen, she knew. She might have preconceived ideas on the solution, but she would listen.

In the meantime, until she could get to Phoenix and the reassuring comfort of Sharon's home, she poured her heart out to a stranger.

But the idea of depending on the kindness of strangers might have suffered some since the days of Blanche DuBois.

Chapter Six

Susan told John good night at the door to her motel room and thanked him for his help. He had carried Bryan in and laid him on the bed while she put Chrissy into the portable crib that had been supplied by the motel staff. Cressman hesitated, looking around. For what, Susan didn't know. She would remember later that her thoughts had been on how kind he was. If she'd had any idea what lay ahead, she would have run in the opposite direction. But there was no indication, no premonition of anything. Her car was immobile, and she lacked the physical energy to run anywhere. And she was completely unaware of even the possibility of danger, so after Cressman left, she undressed and went to bed.

The mattress sank under her. Too many years and too many bodies had slept on it before. That thought was an unpleasant one—similar to placing one's feet into a pair of bowling shoes that who knew how many thousands of feet had been in before—but she felt too tired to care much. Instead she found that, as was always the case, the minute she could relax, her mind went into overdrive, and the most prominent feature in her preoccupation was Kevin. Where was he at that very moment? How many miles separated them right now? Was he safe? She could picture his face, his wide, even eyes that kept a level gaze on her when they talked, his hair dark and thick although he wore it short for the Corps. His nose was a smooth, straight line, and she had the urge to kiss him on the nose at the oddest times. His body remained lean and muscular with the physical training that he went through regularly—so lean, in fact, that she was occasionally surprised by his strength. Susan fell asleep with her thoughts in a fuzzy mixture of love and arguments.

At some point during the night Susan awoke abruptly. Something had awakened her. A noise? Something she could not place in her conscious mind. It nagged at her, just beyond reach. She lay still, the room black on a moonless night. There was no glow at the edge of the drapes, no light in the room at all. For the briefest of seconds she felt her insignificant presence as one small human in a vast, open space, a dot on the planet. A speck. What was she doing here, so far from anything and anyone who cared about her? And anyone who knew where she was?

The room was too quiet. She could hear the sounds the children made in their sleep. The sound of Bryan breathing evenly on the bed across the room was echoed by Chrissy's baby sounds coming from the crib.

Wood creaked, but that didn't alarm her. Old buildings made settling noises all the time, and the motel definitely qualified as an old building. No, it wasn't a noise that alarmed her, but, unexpectedly, her heart quickened.

There was someone in the room.

She wasn't sure what confirmed that thought in her mind. There had been no movement and no audible sound. Was it the sound of breathing over and beyond that of her own and the children's? Susan lay perfectly still, her breath loud in the silent room. She needed to get a hold of her nerves, and in an effort to do that, to literally throw light on her fear, she stretched out her hand and reached for the switch to turn the lamp on.

A hand gripped her wrist and stopped her before she could reach the switch. Susan opened her mouth to yell, but a hand closed over her mouth—a grasp so tight, it ground her lips into her teeth. A heavy body moved onto the bed, and every dark fear her mind had ever harbored rose to the surface. *No!* her mind screamed. She struggled and fought, pushing at any solid body mass her hands came into contact with. She tried to kick, but she felt the thrust of a knee across her body. The weight on her legs pressed into her bones till she thought they would break. Susan reached blindly for a face, for anything she could get her hands on, but she felt nothing. The upper body of who-ever held her down had reared backward out of her reach.

Susan's outstretched arm was wrenched and dragged down beside her legs and forced under the knee of her assailant. Fear rose in her throat like bile and threatened to choke her. Her mind screamed for Kevin. Why had she left the safety of her daily life, the protection of the base? Her free arm came into contact with a face, and she clawed at it with her nails until she heard a groan in response.

The clatter beside her, the sound of fumbling, she mistook as a struggle to find the lamp switch. Instead, a sharp jab stuck her arm, sinking into her flesh. *Hot, stinging pain. A needle? No!* She fought back. *No!*

The pain stopped; the hold on her body loosened. Susan worked one leg loose and brought it up between his knees, but her aim fell short as a warm flush crept upward and flushed outward through her body, extending out to her arms and legs. A vague incoherence, an involuntary relaxation, spread through her mind and released her arms to fall to her sides. Then the weight lifted off her body and settled onto the bed beside her. Her eyelids faltered, wanting more than anything to close, but she dragged them open. *My babies,* was her last conscious thought, *my babies!*

The early-morning flight went off smoothly. The sky, a sharp blue, signaled closure to the mission. Mendoza felt a stiff ache in his arm, but it couldn't compare to the drumbeat of pain in his head. Pain that was the effect of the drinks he and Branni-gan had shared. Brannigan had then displayed a singular lack of manners by appearing at the muster for the return flight in the morning looking for all the world as if he'd never touched a drop and had slept ten hours.

Only at closer range did the tension in Brannigan's face show. What had happened? Mendoza wondered. He knew it was woman trouble, but just how bad was it?

The plane hit turbulence over the Atlantic, and Brayhill began to make noise about it immediately. "I hate it when it does that. I don't even like flying."

Hutton laughed at him. "You sure picked an interesting occupation if you don't like flying."

"I didn't join the Air Force!"

The room solidified around her, coming into focus—large, bright with sunlight, and unfamiliar. Susan searched the room for recognition of something, anything, before she remembered what had happened at the motel. There'd been someone in her room! Where were her children? She jumped out of the bed and winced at the ache of abused muscles. She looked down at her body; she was dressed in her own pajamas, the ones she had put on at the motel. She looked around the room again. Three doors. The first she tried was a massive closet, but what frightened her were the clothes hanging there. They were her clothes and all hung neatly on the hangers; even her shoes were lined up evenly on a shoe rack. Who had put them there? And, more important, why? And where was she?

Susan pulled on the second door and felt like a game-show contestant. *And what do we have behind door number two?* Only this was no game. She opened the door to find a petite wrinkled face staring at her, a very brown face. An Indian? Where was she that had Indians?

"Who are you?" Susan challenged.

Silence. The black eyes watched Susan warily.

"Where am I?" Susan demanded. "And where are my children?"

"*No hablo Ingles,*" the tiny woman answered.

"Where am I? Whose house is this?"

Still nothing. Susan looked over the woman's head into the room beyond. It was another bedroom, but it had been furnished with children's furniture. And there on the far side of the room, lying in a crib, was Chrissy. Susan pushed the woman out of the way and ran toward the crib. She picked her baby up and held her tiny round body close to her own.

"*La leche.*" The woman pointed toward a bottle lying in the crib. The bottle was full.

"She doesn't take a bottle! Where's Bryan? Where's my little boy?"

"*El niño?*"

It was impossible. The woman spoke no English. And understood even less. Susan rushed back into the first bedroom and out the one remaining door. A long hall stretched out ahead of her. Where was Bryan? She heard the sound of footsteps and realized they were coming toward her. Bryan entered the hall with John Cressman holding on to his hand, and Susan stared, unable to speak. A dizzying disorientation came over her. She needed to sit down.

Bryan ran to her and threw his arms around her knees. "Mommy, Mommy!" Susan held onto his sturdy little body, and relief flooded through her, leaving her knees weak. "Did you sleep good, Mommy?" It was a question Susan often asked him. She nodded in reply. "I saw puppies, Mommy, lots of puppies. You want to see them?"

John spoke up for the first time; he told Bryan, "She'll see them in a little while, Bryan. Why don't you go into the kitchen with Maria and get some cookies? I need to talk to your mother." Without his calling her, the diminutive woman came into the hallway, and John gestured to her to take the boy to the kitchen. Bryan was always agreeable whenever cookies were mentioned. His short legs followed the woman happily.

"Did you sleep well?" John asked her.

"Did I *sleep* well? Did I *sleep well?* Are you crazy? What are you doing? Why am I here? You brought me here, didn't you? You broke into my room, and you drugged me!"

"I'm sorry about that. If it hadn't been necessary—"

"Necessary! You call it necessary? And what did you give me? What kind of filthy drugs did you give me?"

"Filthy? Oh, no, it was nothing like that. No, it was just something to knock you out for a while. I studied veterinary medicine."

She gasped. "Veterinary medicine? I can't believe this! And why did you do it? Why did you bring me here? Why?"

"I wanted to help you," Cressman told her.

She laughed out loud, but there was no humor in it. "What are you talking about? What do you mean, you wanted to help me?"

"I saw how unhappy you were. You left your husband. You obviously needed to get away. I want you to stay here. This will be a good place for the children."

"Good for the children! Are you serious?" Susan couldn't believe the audacity of the man. The baby began crying, and Susan bounced her gently, trying to soothe her. "You can't just snatch people and take them off with you. We have a life! I have a husband! And a home!"

Cressman stood resolute. "He hasn't been good to you. You left him."

"What do you know about our lives?" But, even as she said it, she knew that he did know more than he should because she had told him way too much during their dinner the evening before. "I didn't leave him! Not in the sense you mean." The baby cried louder, and Susan's voice rose higher in pitch.

"I can take care of you, Susan. I can give you everything you need. I know it would have been better if we had known each other longer, but there wasn't time. You planned to leave as soon as your car was repaired. I know this isn't the way we should get started, but it'll work out. You'll get used to the idea. And you'll feel better after you've settled in."

Settled in? Susan couldn't believe what she was hearing; a shiver ran along her spine, the first vague suspicion like a distant knell of warning that, perhaps, this man had lost touch with reality. The baby cried louder, and Susan told him, "I'm going to feed the baby now, but I want you to get Bryan and collect all our belongings so you can take us back to the motel. I'll be ready in twenty minutes." With that Susan turned and went back into the room with the crib. She sat down on the rocker and tried to calm down long enough to feed the baby.

Footsteps warned of his approach again; he pushed the door open and loomed in the doorway. For a moment he hesitated, and then he crossed the room until he stood inches from her. He stared deeply into her eyes for a long, silent moment before he reached out and ran one finger across her cheek and down her throat. She shrank from his touch, her mouth went dry, and she felt she would choke.

"I've been lonely here since my wife died." Cressman touched her lips, and she gasped. Her lips parted; she couldn't draw in air, she couldn't breathe.

"You're going to like it here," he said.

Long after he left the room, Susan sat holding the baby. Chrissy had fallen asleep, and her solid, round, baby body lay heavily against Susan. Chrissy's perfect little bow of a mouth moved in her sleep, suckling still in her dream. But it was for Susan's own comfort that she held on to her baby, suddenly afraid that her family was slipping from her fingers.

Chapter Seven

Andrews Air Force Base, situated outside Washington, D.C., lay under the dark clouds of a summer storm. Rain pelted the area during the night and then strengthened during the morning hours in advance of the actual storm front. Brannigan's men hung over the coffeepot and sprawled across chairs as the C-130 refueled to take them on the last leg of their journey. With the mission completed, the long hours of travel wore thin.

The storm broke with surprising strength and sent crewmen scattering for cover. A strong wind surged through the area, created havoc, and left damage on the base and in the nearby community—tree limbs downed, signs banged about, and windows broken. The local flight club lost several light planes; the planes had blown into one another like toys on a playroom floor. And then, of course, came the one thing they'd worried about most: the storm warnings interrupted all departures.

Stalled into inactivity, the men became bored once they caught up on their sleep. Hutton paid a corporal ten bucks to drive him off base in the last hours of the storm. He returned with pizza and beer. He came around the corner of the hangar carrying three large pizza boxes and several six-packs.

Mendoza frowned. "Where have you been?"

"The pizza place." The answer was so innocuous that even Mendoza laughed.

Brayhill slapped a heavy hand down on Hutton's head,

which was nearly bald, cut in the high and tight style Marines favored. "You're crazy, man."

"Wait till the captain catches sight of that beer," Brooks told him.

"What beer?" Brannigan asked. Every one of the men turned at the sound of his voice and snapped to attention.

"At ease." Brannigan stood three feet from Hutton, who still held the six-packs and the pizzas stacked to his chin.

"What beer are you talking about? I'm sure all of you men know that this area is off-limits for beer. Isn't that correct, Sergeant Mendoza?"

"Yes, sir." Mendoza refrained from smiling, but only just.

"Carry on, men." Brannigan turned and left the hangar, restraining the smile that pulled at the corners of his mouth. He envied the easy camaraderie among the men. Sometimes following protocol was a lonely road.

Two hours later the storm blew south, and the waning sunlight returned, breaking out over the area in time to end the day. The men and the equipment loaded the C-130 for the remainder of the journey home.

Susan sat on a hard dining room chair and stared at the food in front of her without seeing it. The shock of waking up in John Cressman's house had overwhelmed her. She had talked until she wanted to scream. And she had fought to get out of the place—with reasoning, with her powers of persuasion, and finally with her physical strength. During the afternoon she stared out the window, trying to work out a way to get free.

On the surface it appeared simple enough. Why not simply pick the children up and leave? Cressman had felt obligated to let her know that the ranch sat three miles back from the road if she walked it, and *if* she knew which way to go, she would have thirteen miles to the town after she reached the gate. Sixteen miles of walking in the relentless heat carrying both children because Bryan's three-year-old legs could never carry him that far. She could hope for a car to come by, but she had seen how little-traveled the road to Fleming was on the side toward the Interstate. No, her only hope was getting hold of a telephone or a car, and in the case of a car, that meant getting hold of the keys too because she had no earthly idea how to hot-wire a vehicle.

The telephone, then. But where was it? Her own cell phone had disappeared from her purse, and she had seen none at all in the huge living room where Cressman had taken her after she fed Chrissy. Neither bedroom had a phone, and now, in the dining room, she looked around surreptitiously for any sign of a phone or connection.

"You'll feel better if you eat something, Susan."

The look Susan gave him was unmistakable in its intent.

"Please, Susan, give it a chance," he said. "You'll like it here."

"I have my own life. I have a husband. A house. Friends. Family. Do you understand what I'm saying to you? I have a life of my own!"

"A life you ran away from," he said with a tone that was annoying because it remained calm.

"I did not run away from my life. I left it for a while," she restated stubbornly.

"You were unhappy," he said.

"I was upset! Everyone gets upset at one time or another."

"Upset enough to drive across the country with two small children in a car that wouldn't hold up to the trip?"

"All right. Maybe I was a little impulsive, even foolish. I should have flown. I wish now that I had." She stared at him, her eyes daggers, her mouth twisted in anger.

"But you didn't, don't you see? There's a reason you didn't, and it's because this was meant to be. It's lonely out here. I love this land, but I need someone to share it with."

"I already have someone to share my life with. I have a husband!" She stated this through gritted teeth.

"He hasn't taken care of you. He leaves you and the children. He doesn't deserve a woman like you."

"It's his job! He has to go where he's sent. It's all a part of his job." How easily she defended the very thing that had so angered her in the past. The irony did not escape her notice.

Cressman continued as though he hadn't heard a word she'd said. "You'll be happy here. Bryan already likes it. Did he tell you about the calf? He wants to name her Daisy."

Susan slumped back against the chair. There was no way to deal with this man rationally. He heard only what he wanted to hear, what pleased him.

"He really likes that calf. I think it was love at first sight." He looked at her with a steady gaze. "Do you believe in love at first sight?"

Susan remembered the first time she'd laid eyes on Kevin. They had met in traffic court, where both were paying tickets. She had noticed him in the next line. He was tall and wore a short-sleeved shirt that revealed well-developed arms. Muscles had never been what drew her to a man, but she did have eyes. Seconds later, while she waited in her line, he turned his blue-gray eyes on her and smiled. Smiles were a different story; smiles that lit up the eyes were impossible to resist. Yes, she believed in love at first sight.

Cressman had continued talking; now she tuned in to what he was telling her. "I couldn't believe it," he continued. "You were such a striking contrast to the barren land around you, blond and beautiful and soft. My wife was blond—did I tell you that?" Susan did not respond, but he stood suddenly and came toward her. He pulled her out of the chair and towered over her, not simply because of his height, but because of his physical bulk. She shrank back in apprehension. His aftershave assaulted her, enveloped her senses, and gagged her. Cressman's hands were large, the fingers broad from years of work on the ranch, and he gripped her arms and squeezed the flesh.

"You look like her," he said, and his face was so close, she could see the lines around his eyes. "You look like her. Not the color of your eyes but the color of your hair and something around the mouth. Your mouth is so much like hers that it shocked me the first time I looked at you." He moistened his lips and stared at her. His eyes held a faraway look, as if he stared into the past instead of the present. Susan lowered her hands to her side to hide the fact that they were shaking. "You're not afraid of me, are you?" He lowered his voice to a whisper. "You have no reason to be afraid of me." There were flecks of green in the blue of his irises, and somewhere within them lay a deep sorrow. "Don't be afraid that I'm going to force you to do anything that you don't want to do. I'll wait for you to come around."

Susan stared into his face. *He'll wait until I come around?* She backed away, but he grabbed her and pulled her close again. He leaned down and kissed her. She had expected a passion bordering on violence, but he kissed her with a tenderness that surprised her.

When he released her, it was so sudden, she staggered backward. He said again, "This won't go any farther until you're ready." He looked strangely uncomfortable, his eyes restlessly circumventing the room before he whispered, "It should have been just the boy. That would have been perfect. Just the boy and the two of us."

Susan stared at him, confused. "What are you talking about?"

His pupils narrowed, focused, and he stared into her eyes. "What? Oh, it's all right. We'll have plenty of time."

Time for what? she wondered, but she was afraid to ask.

Chapter Eight

Whe Brannigan reached their quarters, he found the house silent and dark. It was no surprise because the hour was late. *Good,* he thought, the children will be asleep. Although he was eager to see them, he knew that he and Susan needed time together, time to talk and time to make up. Brannigan said good night to the corporal and climbed out of the jeep. He arched his shoulders and back; he was stiff and sore from sitting so many hours. And he felt tired, tired enough to hope that Susan would be glad to see him and they could avoid discussion altogether till morning.

The doorbell echoed inside the house, but when Susan didn't appear, he bent down and groped under the potted palm for the key Susan kept there. It had been one of the adjustments they'd made when Bryan became fascinated with keys—his interest never included putting them back where they belonged. He crossed the entryway in the dark. The darkened house was expected; lights left on during the night would prompt a letter from the C.O. Brannigan reached for the light and blinked when it illuminated the room. Even his eyes were tired, but a hot shower would rejuvenate him in minutes.

He left his gear downstairs and started thinking about Susan and how she looked while she slept. She would be warm and sleepy, her long blond hair tumbled around her shoulders. Best of all, the look she gave him at those times was so soft, it grabbed him every time. He knew the look she gave him was partly due to the fact that she was sleepy, but it never failed to have an effect on him.

The bedroom door stood open, and he felt for the lamp on the dresser. The light flicked on, and he turned to the bed, but he stopped where he stood. The bed was empty. It was empty not only of a body, warm and willing or otherwise, but the bed was made, the comforter smooth.

"What the—?" Brannigan turned and went down the hall to Bryan's room. His bed was made too, his toys neatly stacked on their brightly painted shelves.

In the baby's room, the crib stood empty, devoid of any blankets or toys, anything but the sheet with baby lambs dancing across a field.

Brannigan ran down the stairs, taking two at a time. There was no sign of Susan in the house. If she had been downstairs, she would have heard him when he arrived. The kitchen was clean, the counters wiped spotless and everything in its place. Nothing, not so much as one dish left out anywhere. He went through the laundry room to the garage, turning on lights as he went. The SUV was gone. Only his car remained, parked in its usual spot.

Bryan loved the ranch; there was no getting around that fact. He loved the horses in the corrals, the new calf, and the fat piglets in the barn, and, most especially, he loved the new puppies. Every opportunity possible he would sit beside the box and hold each one in turn, and he displayed a gentleness and consideration that was way beyond his years.

In the house, a wooden rocking horse appeared on the second day, dusted off and dragged from storage. The sound of the wooden horse could be heard at intervals throughout the day as Bryan took off on imaginary journeys.

Susan sat in the rocker and watched his enjoyment, envious of his carefree spirit. She had no energy, and it occurred to her that it could be the effect of drugs. She wondered if Cressman had drugged her again the night before. Had he slipped something into her food or drink? She had expected to lie awake with the overwhelming responsibility of getting her children out of this place and out of the danger they were in. Instead she'd slept through the night, and she'd slept deeply and without dreams. And when she woke, she felt a lethargy that was not like her normal self.

Susan accused Cressman of drugging her with medication meant for animals.

Cressman looked at her evenly. "I wouldn't do that."

But she knew that he would. And had.

"The baby will get traces of anything I take," she told him, "and it would be very dangerous for her."

"The baby looks fine," Cressman told her.

She had to admit that Chrissy appeared to be all right. She scooted across the floor, reached for toys, and chattered happily in baby talk. Actually, both of the children appeared to be fine. They had their mother with them; they were used to their father being away for weeks, even months, at a time, and they were happily distracted by the new surroundings.

When Susan put the children down for their naps, she sat and stared out the living room window. From where she sat, she could see the front driveway clearly where it swept past the edge of the yard. The problem was that it stretched out of sight in both directions. As far as she knew, either direction could be the way to get off the ranch. While she watched, a man on a black horse appeared from the left and rode off into the opposite direction. Cressman drove up in a pickup truck and spoke briefly to the man when he returned, then drove off, following the man on horseback, off toward the left of the house. The ranch hand had most likely come from the working side of the ranch, and that being the case, the drive to get out of the ranch would be toward the right.

The town, then, according to the sun, was east of the ranch, but the drive was long. Cressman had warned her that the distance to the gate alone was three miles. Could he be lying? There was no way for her to know. If it was that far, it was pointless to try to get away walking and carrying two small children, at least while Cressman was in proximity. The land was sparsely covered, and she would be easy to spot even from a distance.

As the afternoon wore on, depression settled in. Cressman walked in and found her still by the window. "Come on," he told her. "Let's take a ride. I want to show you the ranch."

"I don't want to see it." Susan sounded like a petulant child.

"Now there's no point in sulking. It will do you good to get out." He was not asking; his tone had become inflexible. Susan rose from the chair reluctant to go anywhere he wanted to go. But one purpose would be served; she could get more familiar with the layout of the ranch.

"I want to check on the children first," she insisted.

"The children are fine. They got up from their naps, and Maria is giving them a snack."

"I want to see for myself!" she demanded.

Cressman raised his hands, palms out, as a silent form of . . . what? Submission? Approval? She walked down the hall and opened the door to the nursery and saw both children seated on the floor, Bryan eating a cookie and Chrissy gumming a zwieback cracker. They looked up at her. "Mommy," Bryan called. "Do you want a cookie?"

Susan went to him and kissed him on the top of his head. "No, thanks, buddy. You stay right here with your sister, okay? I'll be right back."

Chapter Nine

Brannigan hadn't moved. He sat in the same chair he'd been in most of the day. And he drank from the same bottle. He'd begun with a glass and ice but had long since dispensed with the niceties. Opening the bottle, he drained it and then sat studying it. His fingers closed around the neck of the bottle, and he threw it across the room. It slammed against a wall, the glass shattered, and liquid sprayed in every direction.

Where was she? It was his one continual, driving thought. When he'd returned and found Susan gone, he had hoped she was out for the evening, but his gut told him differently. When she hadn't returned, he had begun the phone calls. First the few friends they had in the area. By morning he had called friends and relatives, and when he'd had no success at that, he had started drinking. He wasn't normally much of a drinker, but he could not even guess where Susan could be. None of her family and close friends lived anywhere near. He had reached her parents, her brothers, and his own parents, and he'd sounded them out to learn whether they had seen or heard from her. Brannigan tried to reach her sister, Sharon, in Arizona, but no one answered. Nor had his brother, Charles, and his wife, Hannah, both of whom Susan liked very much. Their babysitter had answered and said they'd had an early-morning meeting with the city council. Kevin asked if the children's Aunt Susan had visited recently. The children, quizzed by the sitter, had said no.

The worst part had been to give reasons for his asking without alarming everyone. "I've just returned from a mission, and she'd talked about taking a little trip with the kids while I was gone. She may have taken a short trip around here with her friends and thought she'd be back before I returned."

"Are you sure?" Susan's mother had asked.

"Yes," he'd told her. "I'm sure that's the case, and I'll hear from her soon. I'll have her give you a call later when she gets back."

He thought he had effectively eased out of the situation without causing them to worry. But what about *his* worry? What could he do now?

He paced, trying to think. He sat on the sofa and looked around the living room at the plants, the books, the furnishings, and all the things Susan had bought and arranged. Kevin picked up a book from the table. It was Bryan's *Tommy the Tank Engine* book. Bryan loved trains. Brannigan carried the book into the kitchen, looking for the bottle of Scotch he'd bought weeks before. He knew it was there because he had never opened it and Susan did not like Scotch.

Back in the living room Brannigan poured a glass and looked at *Tommy the Tank Engine*. The train engine's big round eyes looked back at him. The thing that worried Brannigan most was not really fear about Susan's safety; deep in his gut he feared she had left him. The mystery of where she was, by comparison, had become the lesser of his worries. He could find her; he felt that was only a matter of checking around, looking in enough places. But would he find her and then discover that she would not come back to him?

By late morning he had collapsed on the couch in an exhausted heap. His sleep was fitful, with dreams shot through with a frightening sense of loss, and he woke with a headache. He made two more calls as the sun set on the day. This time to Kathy, Susan's closest friend and roommate in college, and Susan's aunt who, he remembered, had become ill before he left. Had Susan gone to take care of her aunt? A kindness such as that was like her. But, no, neither Susan's friend nor her aunt had heard from Susan in a week.

Brannigan felt restrained, restricted somehow; he wanted to strike out in some direction, to take action, but where? How? He got to his feet and pulled his shirt off and threw it to the floor. Then he went out to the kitchen and started to pour himself another drink. But drinking did no one any good—he knew that. Hadn't he told his men often enough? Drinking never solved anything. Then what was he doing? Where was his wife? And where were his children?

His gut feeling that Susan had left him was not openly confirmed until he went through the house checking through Susan's clothes and all the children's things. Not everything was gone, but Bryan's favorite toys were nowhere to be seen, and lots of the kids' clothes and Susan's were gone. The most conclusive proof came when he saw that Susan's luggage was gone. All three of the suitcases—that would be a lot of luggage for a short trip.

Brannigan placed another call to Sharon, Susan's sister, but still no one answered. Surely Susan would not have driven out to Phoenix or to her parents' house, which was even farther.

Night fell, and Brannigan's anger and frustration turned into depression. Finally, physical exhaustion overcame his mental anxiety, and he fell asleep.

A heavy pounding broke into Brannigan's consciousness; the relentless thrumming woke him in the early-morning hours. He lay still, dull and confused for a moment. The pounding proved to be outside his head, but it kept an even tempo with the dull throb in his head. He realized the loud banging was at the door, and he pulled himself off the couch, wincing at the increased pain in his head.

Mendoza's face stared at him once he succeeded in opening the door.

"What do you want?" Kevin grumbled.

Mendoza's eyes opened wide, but he said nothing at first, waiting to be asked in. When nothing was forthcoming from Brannigan, Mendoza said, "May I come in?"

"I'm busy right now." The statement was ludicrous, since it was obviously not true.

"I can see how 'busy' you are. I'd like to come in anyway."

Brannigan shrugged. "Suit yourself." He turned and left Mendoza to shut the door. Mendoza went straight to the phone, lifted the receiver, and punched in a number. "Corporal, this is Sergeant Mendoza. Will you inform Major Dutmer that Captain Brannigan is ill and will be in quarters today? Thank you." He replaced the receiver before turning to look at Brannigan.

"You've got a nerve," Brannigan told him.

"What happened?" Mendoza asked, ignoring the remark.

"None of your business." Brannigan crossed the room and eyed the bottle of Scotch.

"That won't help," Mendoza told him.

Brannigan shrugged.

"It won't change anything."

Brannigan looked at Mendoza and said, "Shouldn't you be working?"

"Yes." Mendoza studied Brannigan, taking in his unshaven face, bloodshot eyes, and wrinkled civvies. "You look terrible."

"Thanks." Brannigan's sarcastic reply was unlike him.

"Are you going to tell me what's wrong?"

"No." Brannigan rubbed his already red eyes and added, "It's none of your business."

Mendoza's eyes narrowed. He looked around. There were no sounds coming from anywhere in the house. "Where's your wife?"

"That's also none of your business."

The two of them stared at each other steadily. Mendoza's clean-shaven, sleep-rested face with the omnipresent tan blended with his perfectly sharp uniform. "You look disgustingly fit and tidy this morning," Brannigan told him.

"I'm not leaving." It was a flat statement, not particularly defiant, simply stating a fact.

Brannigan sat down heavily and acquiesced, accepting Mendoza's presence.

"Where is your wife?" Mendoza repeated.

"Gone." Brannigan refused to look at him, but his face was haggard.

"What do you mean, 'gone'?"

"Gone. Gone! As in not here."

"Did she leave a note?"

"No." Brannigan shook his head. "Not one word."

"Do you know where she is?"

"How should I know where she is? I was on a mission, remember? I came home and found the house empty."

"Did you check the hospital?"

"The what?" Brannigan looked up, chilled by the thought. It hadn't occurred to him that Susan might have been injured somehow or that maybe one of the children was sick. Anything could happen while he was gone, and he hadn't been here much.

Mendoza reached for the phone again and began making calls.

Chapter Ten

The door to the hall opened without sound, and Susan slipped through and walked across and into the dining room. Very little light shone in through the windows. The curtains were sheers—chosen, no doubt, by Cressman's wife. Susan had thought a lot about his wife since she'd been on the ranch, and she wondered if the isolation had worked on Cressman's wife the way it did on her. Maybe she had died of loneliness out here after losing her child. She'd had no other woman to talk to other than Maria, and that was if she spoke Spanish.

Feeling her way along the top of the buffet, Susan felt no phone and no keys. Not too surprising. She'd looked often enough in the daytime. During every meal she scanned the dining room, looking for something, anything, to help her. Susan had narrowed her most-wanted objects down to a list of two: a phone or keys to a vehicle—any vehicle that she could drive off the ranch.

Now, she pulled the drawers in the buffet open and searched through them with the lightest touch of her fingertips, being careful not to shuffle the items around and thus make a noise. She could define most objects with her hands, "seeing" them by touch, but she found nothing useful in the drawers.

When she finished with the buffet, she went into the living room and searched small containers on the bookcase and in the desk over to one side. The desk held almost nothing, as if it had rarely been used. Had it belonged to Cressman's wife? Susan felt the edge of a stack of paper and a few paper clips, nothing more. She moved on and ran her hands along the mantel over the fireplace, the wood rough under the soft pads of her fingers. There was nothing else in the room unless she dug her fingers down in between the sofa cushions.

The kitchen had a wealth of places to search—drawers, cupboards, pantry, little nooks and crannies. Susan went through the places one by one as quietly as possible and then reached up to the top of the fridge and felt along it. Nothing there but it felt spotless, no dust, no grime. Maria was worth every cent Cressman paid her and probably more. Susan ran a hand along the window ledge above the sink, and suddenly the kitchen light came on and blazed overhead. She turned around and found Cressman staring at her.

"What do you think you're doing?"

She was caught, red-faced and red-handed. What could she say? When she said nothing, his tone became angry. "I asked you what you're doing."

Susan turned around completely and leaned back against the edge of the counter, forcing a show of calm. "I wanted a glass of water."

"In the dark?" He didn't believe her.

"I didn't want to disturb anyone."

Cressman crossed the kitchen, pulled a glass from the cabinet to the right of the sink, turned the faucet on, and filled the glass. He handed it to her, but he said, "What are you doing in that shirt?"

Susan looked down at herself to figure out what he was talking about. After her shower she had dressed in a pair of baggy pajama pants and a T-shirt. The pajama pants were pink with tiny white and yellow flowers on them, something her sister had sent for her birthday last year. They'd come with a pink T-shirt that said HOTTIE on it, but it was all too much pink for her taste. Susan had used the T-shirt for a dust rag till it became too grimy, and then she had thrown it away, information she wouldn't share with her sister. "What's the matter? What are you talking about?"

"I'm talking about your shirt. That's *his* shirt, isn't it?" Cressman's tone accused her.

Susan looked at the shirt she wore. It said MARINE across the front. Obviously it belonged to her husband, and she'd worn it to bed many times when he was away from her.

"Don't deny it," Cressman harangued. "It's your husband's shirt." His face had contorted into an angry caricature of itself.

"I don't have any intention of denying it," she said evenly. "Yes, it's Kevin's shirt."

"Take it off!"

Susan hadn't expected him to become so unreasonable. It was a side of him that she hadn't seen except in far more subtle ways. "You're kidding," she said, incredulous.

"Take it off!" he repeated.

"I will not take it off." Susan gave the same adamant tone back to him. She was very aware of having nothing on under the shirt.

"I said, take it off." He raised a hand, and for just a moment she was uncertain whether he was going to strike her or tear the shirt off her forcibly.

Susan sidled away from him to avoid giving him either chance. "I will not take it off."

He stared at her till she worried it was not just the shirt that he focused on. She crossed her arms over her chest and glared at him.

Cressman stared, his face twisted in anger, but soon he backed down. She was so beautiful, her long hair curling around her shoulders and shining with the light above her, like pale gold. Her eyes stared at him, openly angry, but even then he felt he could fall into them and lose himself. He saw her cover herself with her arms, and he was moved by her beguiling modesty. Her feet were bare on the tile floor, and he asked, "Don't you have any slippers?" His voice had changed to concern.

"I do, but I just came for water." She didn't want to tell him that she'd come barefoot in order to keep quiet.

His expression turned soft, and he said, "Even your feet are beautiful." He stared at her toes with longing.

"I'm going to bed." She skirted around the man and headed out of the room.

"Wait," Cressman said. He opened the refrigerator and pulled out a chilled bottle of water. "Take this. It will taste better than our well water." He gave the bottle to her, his eyes resting on her face with an expression of painful melancholy. But he said, "I don't want to see that shirt again."

Susan left the room and headed back to bed. The search for keys or a phone had been fruitless, but as she went, she muttered to herself, "I'm *not* giving up Kevin's shirt. And I'm *not* getting rid of it."

Chapter Eleven

As she looked out on the land, contemplating an escape, Susan pondered the nature of prison, and she was struck with a truth she'd barely considered before that point. And that was that walls alone do not make a prison. Oh, sure, that was something she should have known. In the literal sense of a prison, the walls were the factor most capable of preventing a normal life—walls, bars, barbed-wire fences, electronic gates, and guns. But an individual could easily be imprisoned by other factors, other restrictions, some self-imposed. What about economic factors or even lack of imagination or energy to get out of a position one was mired in? Was a man who worked in a cubicle all day and lived in a tiny apartment all night, traveling from one to the other without variance or imagination, any less a prisoner than some who were behind bars? The only difference was that he *could* break free of the life he'd chosen or that fate had thrown at him.

The vast and unfriendly land imposed its limits on Susan and her small children. She felt imprisoned on the ranch. The land *was* inhospitable, but Cressman had been the one responsible for bringing her to this point and for holding her captive until—what? Until she changed her attitude and wanted to be with him here? As impossible as that seemed, she had begun to think that was his plan.

Cressman pushed the bale forward on the bed of the pickup truck and then hefted in another. The free-roaming steers were suffering. He looked at the sky and mopped his forehead with his red bandana. If the miserly rain dropped an inch or two, the grass sprouts would feed the cattle for another month. If not, well, he'd be hauling hay more often out to the farthest regions of the ranch. He hefted another bale and then motioned Haedecker to join him. Haedecker stacked the final two bales onto the pickup without a word. In fact, Haedecker was a man of so few words, he made Cressman feel like a glib, fast talker from the East.

"Take this load out to number forty and break it up, then check the trough and the depth of the well. I've got some business to tend to in the house."

Haedecker said nothing, but his thoughts ran rampant. He'd seen the woman with the long blond hair and a body any man would give his eyeteeth to get close to. If the business Cressman had to tend had anything to do with her, he didn't blame the man for taking off in the middle of the workday. Haedecker had driven close to the house twice just to get a look at her himself.

Ed, over at the garage, sat with his feet up on the desk. Business was slow, but he wasn't one to complain about that. He'd seen the way of things years ago. The town hadn't grown, at least not enough to speak of, and he had all the same regular customers year in and year out, almost all the same old cars. It didn't matter to him. He'd still come in every day, even if business got worse. To tell the truth, this was where he knew what he was doing. This was where he was meant to be. His kingdom, he thought, and then he laughed, only it came out more like a snort. But everything made sense to him when he was here in his garage.

Ed's eyes dropped to the work order on the desk in front of him, a bill for the replacement of a radiator. He felt twitchy. Not everything made sense, and that discomforted his complacence and confidence in his world. He thought back to the things Cressman had told him. No, not everything made sense.

Chapter Twelve

Stifling heat. Susan woke in the night and breathed deeply. No smoke. It was all right. There was no smoke and therefore no fire. She'd gotten twisted in the sheet that covered her, that was all. She lay still for a few minutes and concentrated on breathing—breathing in, breathing out. She'd gotten the sheet around her too tightly, and she'd panicked.

When she lay back on the pillow, she fought off the old memories. But that never did any good. She'd learned long ago to let them come, let them float toward her without fighting them. So she did. What had been first? The waking. Sleeping peacefully, content, not a care in the world, and then waking to the overwhelming sense of impending danger. What was it? She'd been nine years of age and hadn't recognized the signs—the haze in the air, the scent. She could remember pushing the covers aside and sticking her legs out and touching the cold floor with her bare toes. She was wearing her white pajamas with the pink elephants all over them, elephants in tutus. The floor felt cold all the way to the hall, but when she opened the bedroom door, she saw flames licking up the wall on the opposite side of the hall.

She slammed the door shut and backed up until her bed hit the back of her legs, and she sat abruptly. What should she do? What *could* she do?

The window. She rushed to the window and tried to raise it, but it wouldn't go up. Her mother had painted the room the month before—had the window been opened since then? She tried again. No use. She yelled, but there was no sound in the house except the growing noise of the fire as it devoured the walls.

Ultimately all she could think to do was get as far from the flames as she could. She pulled her teddy bear and her favorite doll with her, and she went into the closet and curled into a ball at the back of the small square space. She clutched Teddy and Nan—her doll named after the smart and resourceful heroine new to her in the Nancy Drew mysteries. What would Nancy do? Nancy had gotten herself out of predicaments. What would she do?

The closet grew hotter, and she could see flames in the room when she put her face close to the gap under the door. The flames were inside her room! She clutched her bear and doll tightly. The heat grew until the closet felt like the oven when she'd tried to make brownies as a surprise while her mother was outside working in her flower garden. Where was her mother now? Where was Sharon? Her brothers?

Susan coughed and looked up. The air was gray above her head. She coughed again, and sweat trickled down her neck. Where was Daddy?

Wood crashed, and glass shattered. The fire was making her room come apart. The closet door ripped open, and a bizarre alien stood over her. He wore a mask over his face and a yellow-green suit, and he was huge! He bent toward her, reached her, and pulled her up into his grip. But then she saw his helmet, and she didn't fight him. She recognized the helmet of the fire department from when Miss Lucchese took her last year along with all the other second-graders to see a fire station and a fire truck.

Susan had clung to the fireman as he swung around out of the closet toward the window, which he slammed his boot against to widen the hole he'd made to come into the room. As they advanced through the window, she dropped her teddy bear, but the fireman never hesitated; in one fluid movement he swept the bear up and jumped from the window with all three of them in his arms, safe and sound.

She never forgot that night and the fireman who'd saved her, but it took long weeks before she could sleep more than five feet from her parents at night.

Sharon waited, but no word came from her sister. She couldn't believe Susan would drive across two-thirds of the country alone with such small children. What had motivated her to do such a thing?

Jimmy ran into the room, his sneaker-clad feet squeaking across the tile floor. The Saltillo tile made a hard, cold surface, but its orange color warmed the look of the floor and the room. "Mommy, there's a man at the door."

"Where's Rosalinda?" Sharon asked. She pushed Jimmy's hair off his forehead. His pale skin dotted with freckles never failed to make her feel guilty, a reminder of the day she'd kept him out in the sun too long while she scoured yard sales for what she called near-antiques.

"She's at the door with the man."

"Well, Rosalinda will call if she needs us." No sooner had she said it than Rosalinda came into the den.

Rosalinda's soft, dark eyes were shadowed and fearful. She said, "A telegram. For you." In Rosalinda's world a telegram could only be bad news. She handed it to Sharon.

"Thanks, Rosa. You can go back to what you were doing." Sharon pulled open the top desk drawer and searched for her letter opener as Rosalinda turned to leave the room. Jimmy, following his mother's lead, opened and shut desk drawers, banging them closed with too much force.

"Oh, Rosa, will you take Jimmy to the kitchen and give him a snack?"

"Yes, ma'am." Rosa held out a hand, and Jimmy took hold of it and went with her willingly. The word *snack* had prompted his obedience.

"Make it something healthy, Rosa, no matter what he pleads for."

A telegram? Who sent telegrams anymore? Why not just call? Sharon ripped open the envelope and read the brief message.

Chapter Thirteen

The ranch covered 265 acres, nowhere near the largest in West Texas but large enough to get lost in. Cressman showed Susan the land he owned with pride, oblivious to the fact that her only interest remained bent on learning the layout in order to make an escape. The ranch was as well cared for as the house. In their tour they passed several men close at hand, but Cressman displayed no interest in introducing her. She wondered if they knew she'd been brought to the ranch against her will. What story *had* he told them?

Cressman caught her staring at the ranch hands. "They're all first generation up from Mexico and don't speak any English. None. When I talk to them, it's in Spanish. My foreman too. They don't go anywhere else much, so they get by okay."

Susan believed they didn't go anywhere. Where was there to go? The sun beat down on the land and bleached everything in sight. The rocks, the soil—everything reflected the bright sunlight. The air conditioner in the truck blew enough to keep their faces dry, but Susan's back was sticky with perspiration against the seat.

"This will all be his someday," Cressman said in his low drawl. "He's too little to appreciate it now, but you can see what it would mean to inherit this."

"What are you talking about?"

Cressman looked at her. "The ranch. I don't have anyone.

Oh, maybe a distant cousin or two. But this will be Bryan's one day."

"Bryan's?"

"Don't." He grasped her wrist. "Don't try to persuade me to do otherwise. It will be Bryan's." He spoke with a finality that ended further discussion. She wondered if he was obsessed or certifiable.

Several ranch hands worked nearby, stacking bales of hay onto a pickup; two others herded horses into a corral. Susan felt as if she'd stepped into another time, another life, some kind of parallel existence.

"This is best, Susan," Cressman continued on his favorite theme. "It's the best thing for the children and for you."

"What about their father?" she asked him.

"What could he give them?"

"His love," she said belligerently.

"When he's around," Cressman said. "When he happens to be available."

They had returned to the house, and Cressman swung the truck toward the side of the barn that stood some fifty feet from the house.

"That isn't fair," Susan told him. "You don't know what he's like. You don't know anything about our life."

"Don't I?" he asked.

She knew he remembered everything she'd told him in the café that first night, the night he had helped her when her car broke down. She should never have confided in him. He was a stranger, but he had been kind to her. How could she have known?

Cressman stopped the truck near the garage, and Susan craned her neck to see if there were other vehicles inside.

"Two Ford trucks and the Cadillac, and they're all locked. And I have the only keys. Does that answer your question?"

"I didn't know I had asked one," she said with sarcasm, but her heart sank because that was exactly what she'd been wondering.

They stared evenly at each other, Susan determined not to turn away first.

A man appeared at the side of the truck and drew Cressman into conversation. They spoke in rapid Spanish, and Susan watched them. She was certain it was the same man she had seen with Cressman from the window earlier. He stood a head shorter than Cressman, and he was lean and sinewy. She decided that his skin had darkened from working in the sun rather than from any genetic dictation at birth. He glanced toward Susan several times until Cressman's voice rose, and the man turned on his heel and left as quickly as he had come.

"That's Crabb," Cressman told her, "my foreman." He opened the door for her but barred her way as she stepped from the truck. Cressman rested his hands on either side of her waist, sliding them upward and then gripping tightly. She was hot and sticky, and his hands felt heavy and warm against her rib cage. He leaned in closer, but all he said was, "There aren't many women on the ranch. Stay away from the men, and stick close to the house."

What was that supposed to mean? She tried to ask him, but he turned and pulled her back to the house.

Another day gone, and Kevin had come no closer to finding Susan. He sat and watched Mendoza talking on the phone. Mendoza had been tireless, but Brannigan suspected that even Mendoza was running out of ideas. Every known member of Susan's family had been contacted, with one exception. They still hadn't reached Susan's sister. And Brannigan's hope had begun to falter. Sharon was known in the family to be ever busy, always running here and there, but in this day of instant communication, why couldn't he reach her? Was it possible that Susan and Sharon were together somewhere? But, the question was, where?

A hot shower and a shave along with a change of clothes had helped Brannigan, but the best help had been when he rid himself of the depression and the alcohol and began to take action. All of the local hospitals had been checked, and if Susan or one of the children had been admitted to the base hospital, Brannigan would have been notified. Nothing turned up. No clues. He remembered the suitcases and told Mendoza that that was his proof that she'd left him. Mendoza refused to allow Brannigan to do anything but think positively.

When Mendoza hung up the phone, he sat deep in thought.

"What is it?" Brannigan asked.

"Kellerman says your papers for an emergency leave are being cut. I was just wondering if I should—"

Brannigan stopped him. "No. Let's leave it at this. Besides, it's irrelevant right now. We don't even know which direction to take."

"We will," Mendoza told him. "How long since you tried her sister's house?"

Brannigan looked at his watch. "About three hours."

Mendoza looked at his own watch. "It's five in Arizona. Let's give it another hour or two, then we'll try again. That will give them time to get home from work or whatever. In the meantime, let's get a bite to eat."

"Why don't you go home and eat with your wife? I'll just open a can of something. I don't really feel like going out."

"My wife is at a meeting, and I have to fend for myself, so if you don't want to go out, I'll open a few cans for both of us."

Brannigan watched Mendoza disappear into the kitchen. His story sounded fishy. "What sort of meeting?"

Mendoza called out from the kitchen, "Wives club, what else?"

"They meet in the daytime."

"This is a special meeting." Mendoza dropped a pan. "Something about more equipment for the day care. I don't know. Who knows what they do?"

The phone rang, and Mendoza appeared in the kitchen doorway. Brannigan picked up the receiver and answered. "Captain Brannigan."

"Cap'n Brannigan, this is Linda Hoskins over at the base

library. Will you remind Mrs. Brannigan that I'm still holding that book she wanted?"

"Yes, I'll tell her." He shook his head at Mendoza, who then went back into the kitchen.

After a dinner of canned soup and lukewarm peaches, Brannigan picked up the phone and dialed the Phoenix number again. On the second ring he realized he was holding his breath, and he let it out slowly. By the third ring he and Mendoza faced each other, braced for yet another disappointment.

"Hello."

It took a few seconds before Brannigan realized someone had answered. A very young someone. "Hello. Jimmy? Is this Jimmy?"

"Yes. Who are you?"

"Is your mother there?"

"Yes. Mama!"

Kevin swallowed and looked at Mendoza. This could be it. Good news or bad. He felt sick, worse than when he'd been drinking.

"Hello." Sharon's voice came on the line.

"Sharon, this is Kevin."

"Kevin? How are you? Are you back home, then?"

"I need to ask you something," he began.

"About Susan? When I talked to her, she said—"

His heart kicked into a rapid drumbeat. "You talked to Susan? When was that?"

"I don't remember, but she said—"

"Sharon, listen to me. This is important. I have to know exactly when you talked to her. I mean, which day was it?"

"I don't remember, Kevin."

"Think about it, Sharon! I have to know. Think."

"You're scaring me, Kevin. What's wrong? Has something happened to Susan?"

"I can't find her anywhere. She's gone, and the children are too. It's as if they disappeared."

"Oh, that can't be. She was a little upset, but Susan is a very responsible person. You know that."

"I know. And that's the one thing that's got me puzzled. This isn't like her at all. That's why I have to find her. I have to talk to her."

"All right, let me think. I don't know which day it was, but it was the day you left."

"The same day? Are you sure?" He looked at the calendar. That was days ago.

"Yes, the same day. I remember because she said you had just left a few hours before. And that you two had argued and she wanted to come out here."

"She was leaving me." He said it more to himself than to her.

"No. Well, yes. But not like you mean. Oh, I don't know, Kevin. I don't think she was talking about anything permanent. She was upset, and she had packed."

She was packed and ready to leave within hours after he left. He couldn't believe it. What had he said to drive her that far? "What else did she say?"

"Not much. We just talked a few minutes more. I tried to change her mind about driving out here, but she was determined."

"Driving? You mean she wanted to come by car?"

"Yes. And she did too—or at least she started out by car."

"What do you mean, she 'started out'? Have you heard from her since then?"

"Yes. Three days ago. I received a telegram, of all things, and it said that she had changed her mind about coming."

"Do you mean she changed it completely? Or she decided not to come by car?"

"Yes. Yes to the first thing. She decided not to come at all. She said she'd write soon. That's all. It was when we received the telegram that we decided to go ahead with the plans we'd made before. We went up to Flagstaff for a few days."

"You haven't heard anything more from her?"

"No. Nothing. Not a word. I figured she'd call when she wanted to talk."

"You'd tell me if you had?"

"Of course I'd tell you." There was a pause, then Sharon added, "But, I've been worried. She's always been independent, so I didn't want to pry. But she would never disappear without a word, and then that telegram. I doubt she had ever sent a telegram in her life. Why didn't she just pick up the phone and call? Or use her cell phone, for that matter? Maybe she forgot her charger? It's odd, isn't it?"

"Yes, I agree. It is odd." He tried to think, to find reasons for it, for all of it.

Sharon tried to reassure him. "Do you think she's just gone somewhere to sort things out? Or do you think something's happened? Should we call the police?"

"I don't know what to think. But she left on her own. I just need to find her." Brannigan ran his fingers through his hair. He needed a haircut. The thought came automatically, unbidden. He didn't wear his hair as tight as the enlisted men. Susan liked his hair longer. She'd told him so many times, but he'd never confessed that that was the reason he wore it longer— not to Susan, not to anyone.

"When she calls, be sure to let me know." Sharon's concern was evident.

Kevin promised to do just that.

Chapter Fourteen

Mandy sat on the floor and stocked the lowest shelf of canned goods, a job she'd begun to detest. Working at her grandparents' grocery store provided money for the extras she wanted. She was grateful for the money, but would it hurt to have a little fun on a job? She didn't know which was worse to stock, the bulky cereal boxes or the heavy cans. At any rate, she finished the stocking and dusted off her jeans, pushing the cart with boxes toward the other end of the store.

Matt stood in the middle of the aisle and watched her, his long legs covered with tight, faded jeans.

"Hi, Matt. You shopping for your mom?"

"Yeah." He stared at her smooth skin and blond curls. "What time do you get off?"

"Not till seven." Mandy wrinkled her nose to display her opinion of her work hours. When Matt said nothing more, Mandy told him, "See ya."

"Yeah," Matt echoed, "see ya." He watched her walk away, the movement of her body, and he was disgusted for losing his nerve again; he pulled four boxes of macaroni-and-cheese from a shelf and walked off.

Mandy pushed the cart into the back room and left it, then went out to collect an order that needed to be filled. She looked at the order in her hand and then back at the name at the top. What did John Cressman want with diapers? Medium-size diapers. And Cheerios. And bananas. Not his usual order.

Mandy shrugged and pulled a cart from the line of shopping carts crammed together.

Later she asked, "Grandma, does Mr. Cressman have any grandbabies?"

"Not that I know of. What made you ask that?"

Mandy held out the paper with the list on it. "Just wondered, 'cause he's got diapers on his list."

"Oh, well, maybe he's got visitors. Did you finish the order? There's another from the Double Y ranch."

"Yeah, okay." Mandy took the list and pushed off with an empty cart. *Fill this order. Fill that order. Stock the shelves.* What would it be like to work somewhere fun? Like in a mall, in a real city?

Susan set Bryan up on the high chair in the kitchen to trim his hair. His hair was soft to the touch and had a tendency to curl under in the back. Her own hair was held up on the back of her head in a big clip. The metallic snip of the scissors was the only sound other than Chrissy's baby sounds where she sat in her carrier on the floor beside them. Outside, the sun bleached the landscape white, cattle moved slowly in the distance, and time passed in minuscule ticks of the clock on the wall.

One of the ranch hands pulled up in a truck near the house. The man climbed out and started for the door, but someone out of Susan's sight called him. He walked off toward the right and left the truck. For three ticks of the clock Susan looked at the truck without a response, the scissors in midair, and then her brain processed the sound. The truck had been left with the engine running. He'd even left the door open. With no clear and conscious decision, she bent and picked up the baby seat with Chrissy and took Bryan by the hand, pulling him down from the chair.

The back door closed behind them, aided to silence by her foot. Susan circled the truck, and when Bryan opened his mouth to ask where they were going, she whispered, "Shh, we're going to play a game."

Susan hefted Bryan up into the truck and then climbed in, holding the baby. The driver of the truck was in view and speaking to one of the other ranch hands. Neither of them had seen her yet. She closed the door just enough to make it click, and she pushed the shift into gear. The men spotted her, one of them yelled, "Hey!" and they started toward her. Susan stomped on the accelerator, nearly stalling the engine, but the old truck lurched forward and forced the men to get out of her path.

The truck roared around the side of the house and spit gravel at the men. *Which way? Which way?* she thought, and then she chose a direction and followed it until the gravel drive petered out and she hit the natural dips in the land.

The ranch hands yelled and chased after her, but there was little they could do on foot. Susan turned the truck and bounced over the rutted land back toward the drive. The kids began to cry, first Chrissy and then Bryan, but Susan could not stop to comfort them. She *had* to get them off the ranch. That was all she knew. The wheels of the truck went into a rut and stuck. She floored the accelerator, and the truck jumped out of the dry rut and bolted forward.

Her babies continued to cry, and she tried to comfort them verbally with her best soothing-mother's tones. "Shh, it's all right. Don't cry. We're just going through bouncies." She tried several times, but nothing worked. The one thing that would comfort them would be if she stopped the truck and held them on her lap. And, oh, how she wanted to do just that; she wanted nothing more than to do that, but it was for their sake that she couldn't.

A cloud of dust appeared in the rearview mirror, the dust spun up by a vehicle made diminutive by distance but growing as it approached. Susan didn't wonder even for a minute who was coming. She didn't have to ask, even if there had been anyone around to ask.

She had to get out of there—fast.

Chapter Fifteen

The cloud of dust approached at a rapid pace, and Susan jammed the accelerator against the floorboard and veered away from its path. She turned right and then left, remembering that a zigzag pattern made it more difficult to be followed, never mind the old adage that the shortest route between two points is a straight line. Following a line, straight or otherwise, would be difficult in the West Texas terrain.

The truck took a dip into a ravine, and for a while the roll of land covered them from Cressman's sight. The solid bulk of earth felt like an embrace and gave the illusion of safety. *Please, God, may we stay this way, enfolded by the warm arms of the earth?* But, as luck would have it, the ravine foreshortened and then ended altogether, and the truck rose back into sight and barreled across the rock-strewn land.

The children bounced and jiggled as Susan pushed the old truck as fast as she dared, avoiding the larger rocks in their way. The baby was all right in her carrier on the floor, and she pinned Bryan behind her right shoulder and held him there. The cloud of dust that had obscured Cressman's truck diminished or at least lifted enough for plain sight. The truck drew close enough for her to recognize Cressman's Stetson. He'd been to town; he never wore his genuine Stetson except for dress occasions. How it disheartened her to realize he'd been gone and had the sense of timing to return to the ranch just when the opportunity presented itself for their escape.

The two pickup trucks played cat-and-mouse tag, hitting bumps, jagging around boulders. She did not like the image of herself as the "mouse" in this dangerous chase. Cressman stayed so close, Susan expected at any moment to feel the slam of his bumper against the rear of the truck. She forced the old truck to top speed, leaving the newer truck behind temporarily, but just as she crested a rise, the solid earth beneath her gave way to open space, and the truck took a nose-dive into a gully. The dry-as-a-bone gully had been created by water runoff from the once or twice a year that heavy rain fell.

The truck had stopped, nose down, rear in the air, and the engine died. She tried to spark the engine into life, but nothing happened. Chrissy looked up at her now from the passenger side floorboard. Susan reached for her to pull her up onto the seat, but before she could get her up, the door beside her was ripped open, and Cressman accused her, "What's the matter with you? Are you crazy?"

She looked at him. He stared at her with what appeared to be genuine concern as he stood there with his long legs balanced, one on the wall of earth and the other in the ravine. "No," she said unkindly, "that's your department."

Cressman froze; the expression in his eyes altered instantly. He was hurt. Her words had wounded him, but she couldn't let herself care. She turned back to lift the baby's seat up, but Cressman yanked her out the door and stood her on the uneven ground. She immediately fell back onto her rear. He never offered her his hand; he reached into the cab, picked both children up, and turned and walked off. All that was left to Susan was to dust off the seat of her pants and scurry after him to his truck.

At least she was safe, Brannigan thought. She *had* to be safe—she was where she wanted to be, wherever that was—but he wouldn't be satisfied until he could speak with her. He would not let her go easily. Hadn't he learned enough about loss with Ethan? His brother had been nine years old to his own age of seven when the two of them had walked to the river's edge during a family campout. Heavy rain during the night had left the river swollen and swift. Debris floated by at a dizzying pace as they threw sticks into the water to watch them and leaves still green that had been washed from the trees in the rain. The river carried mud down from higher ground, but when they pooled some of it in tin cans, the water sparkled clear. The air around them was equally clear, washed fresh by the rain. The trees overhead were a very bright green from the more-than-abundant rainfall, and the sun shone down on the two of them and created an ideal day in which to play.

Which of them first had the idea to build a raft was something that was blurred by time, perhaps by a mixture of time and guilt. They'd spent months reading about the adventures of Tom Sawyer and Huck Finn, reading each night with their mother, and the tales of living on and by the river had created a magical world.

They collected branches that were too slender for a raft, but it was not the strength of the raft that had caused the tragedy. Ethan had moved nearer the riverbank to collect branches; he bent to pick one up, and then he was gone.

The guilt surfaced occasionally even now, all these many years later, but Kevin had tried to help. He'd run to the river's edge, grasping a long branch for Ethan to grab hold of, but Ethan had disappeared into the rapidly moving water altogether. Not one word of reproach had ever been aimed at him, but, being the only other person nearby, Kevin took the inability to save his brother very hard and felt it had been ingrained into his very soul. The entire family had lived with the loss, but he seemed to have felt it the deepest. In some ways it directed his future, because from that day forward he had tried his very best to please his parents. To make up for the loss of one son, he had tried to be everything they wanted him to be. A heavy burden for a seven-year-old, but it had eased some in his adult years. But no matter what he did or what he accomplished—even choosing a military life like his father—he couldn't ease their suffering or his own.

Now, faced with the possibility of loss again, he doubted he could bear it. He knew one thing for certain: he would not go gently into acceptance. He would fight with everything he had in him.

Chapter Sixteen

At the midnight hour, the house was silent and dark. One lone, slender shaft of moonlight shot through the open draperies at an angle. Susan moved across the room to where the children lay sleeping. She made no sound. The knob turned easily in her hand, and she hesitated for a minute to allow her eyes time to adjust to the darker room.

Maria was asleep on the cot in a corner. The house was so quiet, Susan could hear Maria's breathing as she crossed the room to the crib. The one thing that would make her plan workable was the baby sling. Susan laid it in the crib and tucked Chrissy into it, then lifted it gently around and onto her back. She had only used the baby sling a few times, and then mostly while she shopped. Chrissy had just about outgrown it. One more night's use was all Susan wanted—one more all-important night's use.

With the baby papoose-style on her back, Susan picked Bryan up carefully. She tensed, knowing this was the crucial moment, fearful that he would wake. Although he stiffened briefly, subconsciously aware of something going on, he settled against her shoulder, his face against her neck, her scent familiar and comforting to him. Bryan's weight pulled at her neck and arm muscles; he was heavy in slumber.

Susan turned toward the door and heard a creak from the cot. She looked back toward the corner and gasped softly. Maria, up on one elbow, stared at her. Their eyes met for one moment, one gut-wrenching, breath-stopping moment, and then, slowly, deliberately, Maria turned over and gave every indication of going back to sleep.

Relief flooded through Susan's bones, even though she knew she had a long way to go to feel any real sense of safety. The hall and the large open living room blurred around her. There was no sound anywhere in the house. The back door kept her for an eternity as she fumbled with the lock before turning the knob in tiny increments, in infinitesimal degrees. At last it gave, and the door came open.

The night air hit her, and she felt encouraged by the success she'd experienced so far. Turning, she crossed the lawn and hit the crunch of gravel on the drive heading in the direction she believed to be the way out. Her back ached before she had gone twenty feet, but she was determined to walk as far as she had to and all through the night, if necessary. She would not be a victim of anyone's psychotic fantasies.

The road stretched before her, uneven and dark. She stumbled once and nearly lost her balance when she stepped into a rut. The children slept on undisturbed as the sounds of the night surrounded them. The ranch was far from any noise that humans made, but Susan heard creatures slithering and rustling through the shrubs. She could not think about that, or she would lose what small amount of nerve she had. In the distance a bizarre howling began and floated on the air, raising the hair along her neck and arms. Were there wolves in the area? Or coyotes?

Moonlight lit the way along the unpaved drive. Susan had chosen a good night for walking off the ranch. She had to get away this night while there was still enough moonlight to see by. Perspiration broke out on her face and ran down her neck; the physical exertion combined with the body warmth of the children slowed her considerably. Her breath grew ragged and loud; she was surprised that the children continued to sleep through it all.

Susan lost track of how long she had walked or how far she

had gone. Still no gate in sight. Why build the house so far from the road? How could anyone want to be that alone?

She saw a curved shadow lying across the road and stopped in midstride. She stood motionless and remembered from her days at girls' camp one instruction: it was important not to move. She worried that her ragged breathing alone was enough to startle the snake. Time passed—how little or how much she could not tell—and the snake didn't move. She inched to the right, thinking she would skirt around it. From the right she gained a better perspective and saw that the end of the snake stuck out in three sections. Never in her life had she heard of a snake with three tails. It was a branch! Relief flooded her, and she forced her feet to move, glad there'd been no one around to view her mistake. She could almost laugh at herself. Almost.

Light flashed in the distance and danced brilliantly across the sky. Her spirits dipped lower. Surely it wouldn't rain. Rain didn't come often in this country. All of the land she'd seen had been so arid and dry that it blew away in the wind.

The night air grew still, like the calm before an approaching storm. And this on the one night of her life that she needed desperately for the weather to cooperate. The previous night had been her first opportunity to escape because the moonlight was so bright, but she had waited. She had hoped to lull Cressman into a false conviction that she had relaxed and accepted the situation. She worried that he had been slipping some concoction into her food or drink, but she could not avoid all nutrition. She made a point of eating only what he ate and serving herself directly from the same bowls. And she drank from sealed bottles or from the communal pitcher. All her strength was needed if she hoped to get the three of them out.

The road ahead curved around a huge boulder. The ragged silhouette flashed in relief when white-hot veins of lightning cut across the sky. The wind struck her in the face as soon as she skirted around the rock, and she could smell the moisture in the air. Little more than a mist, but it was there. Fatigue had etched itself into every muscle, becoming a permanent part of her personal makeup, her metabolism. She remembered a time early in their marriage when she and Kevin had gone out to jog together. They chose a track designed for that purpose, then jogged all the way home. She had begun to look forward to it each day. Her muscles had been toned by the exercise. She remembered one cold evening they had raced to the door and down the hall to the shower, laughing. She'd told Kevin that, because it had been a tie, they'd both won the right to the first shower.

Where was Kevin now, she wondered. What would he think when he came home and found the house empty? She should have left a note, but every thought formulated in her mind had become so much worse when she visualized it on paper. Tears stung her eyes, and, though she knew crying would not alleviate her situation, she allowed herself to indulge in a little self-pity anyway.

Another memory surfaced, of something that had occurred on a cold November day. It had rained all day long, and Susan had been inside with two sick kids. In the gloom of the gray weather she'd felt like she was stuck terminally within the four walls, unable to get out. Kevin had come home from work in mud-encrusted boots. He'd been on maneuvers out in the field, and, glad to get in out of the cold rain, he'd forgotten to remove his boots. Susan discovered him several steps inside the door, tracking mud into the hardwood floors that she had mopped during the one thirty-minute period of the day when both children were asleep. Her expression of dismay and disbelief stopped him, and an argument flared up. Angry words were hurled back and forth between them as he leaned down to remove his boots.

Once he got them off, he crossed the living room and accidentally dropped one of the boots on the beige carpet, adding fuel to Susan's anger. She said, "If you spent your entire day cleaning up after children, you'd be more careful, Kevin."

"It was an accident," he said, exasperated.

The two of them scrambled around on the floor, trying to

scrub first the carpet, and then the floor. Kevin took the still-muddy boots out to the laundry room, where he placed them on top of the dryer after first spreading newspaper across the top of the machine.

Susan continued to scrub the carpet until none of the mud was visible, but she knew it would still stain; the dampness would attract dirt off the bottoms of shoes. Her own feet were covered with big white socks; she still wore the dress she'd put on in the morning when she'd thought she'd need to take the children to the doctor. The socks had been an afterthought, added to keep her toes warm as she moved through the house cleaning and tending the children.

As she got up off the floor, her back ached, and she realized she was tired. Now that she thought about it, hadn't it been *her* bad day that she'd been taking out on Kevin? Why had she done that? He'd been out in the rain and the cold, leading his men on maneuvers all day. That couldn't have been fun. Susan had checked on the children and found Bryan still watching cartoons and Chrissy rolling on the floor nearby, and then she went in search of Kevin. She found him in the laundry room, cleaning his boots. Susan leaned against his back and put her arms around his waist. Kevin stopped what he was doing. She told him against his back, "I'm sorry." Kevin unclasped her hands from his waist and turned to face her. "I had a terrible day, but I didn't mean to take it out on you," she said.

He looked down at her, but he didn't reply; he touched her face gently, and then he picked her up and set her on the washer, bringing their eyes level. For a long moment he looked at her, and then he kissed her. For a makeup kiss, it was all that it could be and more. The kiss lengthened and deepened and ultimately turned into more. When he leaned closer, she wrapped her legs around his middle. Beside them they heard footsteps. "Mommy? Bugs Bunny is bwoken. I want to see moah Bugs Bunny."

Susan and Kevin looked at each other and smiled. "Yes, Bryan. Let's go fix Bugs Bunny."

The memory was sweet now, and quite suddenly Susan cried harder. She cried because of the anger that she and Kevin had allowed to come between them, and she cried for that breathless excitement of just being together that they'd let slip away. Was it over? Or had they only reached the point in their marriage where it would no longer come so easily? The point where they would have to work to stay together?

Rain began to fall—not the gentle rain of her West Coast childhood but huge drops that fell on her head and face, each drop making itself felt on her skin. The drops fell faster and faster until it became a heavy torrent unlike any rain she had ever experienced. The water poured onto her head and into her eyes and streamed onto the children. Susan felt as if her skin was being flayed. Bryan woke up crying in fright, followed by Chrissy, who began to howl. Susan looked around for some kind of cover for them, anything to protect them from the constant barrage of drops pounding their heads and bodies.

The nearest cover, in fact the only shelter, was an outcropping of rock at the foot of a hill twenty feet away. Susan rushed toward it and tried her best to soothe the children, but the deluge drowned out her voice with its roar. All three of them were completely soaked by the time she reached shelter.

A concave indention in the hillside left just enough space for Susan to gather her children underneath. They continued to cry, but she drew them close, hoping to warm them with her own body. All she could do was sit out the storm as it vented its fury on the land around them.

Chapter Seventeen

In the early morning Kevin Brannigan sat and stared into space. Mendoza had gone home hours before, and Kevin found he was unable to take any action. Nothing made sense. Susan had never been the type to make sudden or irrational decisions, and even the idea of a telegram was out of character for her. He couldn't stop thinking about it or trying to make sense of it. Why would she take the time to look up a Western Union office, most likely have to ask for directions to it, and then drive to it in order to send a telegram, when she could simply pick up a telephone and call her sister? Phones were readily available, more accessible than Western Union offices. She had a cell phone of her own. Even e-mail was easier than sending a telegram. That could be done at any local library. No, it didn't make sense. Like a Rubik's Cube or a Cubist painting, no matter how you looked at it, the more it didn't make sense. He had awakened at 5:30 with that thought, and it would not let him alone. A shower and shave and two cups of coffee later and the thought persisted, eating at him. Should he call the police? But where? And which ones? Since she'd left on her own, would they refuse to do anything about the fact that she was still gone? And if he could convince them that she was really missing, wouldn't he be the first suspect? And somewhere deep in his thoughts was the belief that he could, with his expertise, find her himself.

Mendoza arrived at 8:00 looking much less haggard than Brannigan, and the moment he stepped in the door, Kevin told him what he'd been thinking. And like anyone struggling with a puzzling problem, he repeated it again.

"Sometimes people do things that are out of character." Mendoza's expression suggested that Brannigan was grasping at slim possibilities and that he felt the responsibility to make Brannigan aware of that fact.

"No, they don't, or at least not often, and some people never do." Brannigan hesitated, then blurted out exactly what he'd been feeling. "I think something's wrong."

"Maybe you just—" Mendoza began.

"I know. I know what you're going to say, and it's true. Maybe I don't want to face the possibility that Susan left me. I'm not ready to accept that, but my gut tells me that something is out of kilter, something is wrong."

Mendoza studied Brannigan's face carefully, and the silence lengthened between them. Finally he said, "Tell me again what the telegram said."

Brannigan had showered and shaved and dressed in clean jeans and a black T-shirt that said MARINE across the front in scarlet letters. He was young enough to bounce back from the ravages of lost sleep and worry, but the last vestiges were still evident, red lines in the whites of his eyes that were impossible to hide and difficult to erase. He leaned forward, intent on what he was saying. "The telegram said that she had changed her mind, that she was not coming, and that she would call soon. Other than that—" Brannigan stopped in midsentence. "Wait—" he said, reaching for the phone. He punched in numbers, then tapped his fingers nervously while he waited for an answer.

"Sharon, I want you to look at that telegram and find out where it originated."

"Where it originated? You mean, where it came from? They do that?"

"Yes. I want to know where it came from. It should say somewhere on the telegram. Can you take a look and tell me? I'll wait."

"Kevin, I don't even know if I even still have it. I'll look for it. Maybe it's in the stack of papers on my desk, since I haven't cleared my desk in weeks. I'll have to call you back." She hung up.

Brannigan paced the living room floor while Mendoza pulled a carton of orange juice from the refrigerator. He poured a glass for each of them and made toast and buttered it. He smiled as he did this; his wife would be surprised if she saw him, since he rarely did such things at home. Mendoza took the juice and toast to the living room, and they sat down to wait for the return call. Fifteen minutes passed, but Brannigan would later swear that it took an hour for Sharon to return his call.

When the phone rang, he lunged at it and grabbed it off the cradle, as if it were a competition, even though no one else was trying to get it.

"I'm sorry I took so long, Kevin. I went through everything on my desk. What a mess. Old bills. Receipts. Then I remembered. I had thrown it away, but fortunately it was in the wastepaper basket by the corner of my desk. Shows what a great housekeeper I am, doesn't it?"

"What does it say?" Brannigan had no patience for chitchat.

"Well, it says that it's from someplace in Texas. Some town called Pecos. Have you ever heard of it?"

"Pecos, Texas!" Brannigan repeated. It might as well have been Zimbabwe or Mars. "Pecos, Texas?"

"Have you heard of it?" Sharon asked.

"Vaguely. It's somewhere out in West Texas, near El Paso, I think."

"Why would Susan be in Pecos, Texas?"

"That's the big question. That's just what I'm wondering. And what in Pecos, Texas, would make her change her mind about going to visit you? She'd already traveled more than half the distance."

"It's strange, Kevin, but there must be some logical reason for it."

"Then can you clue me in, because I sure would like to know what it is." He didn't even try to contain his anger. What would Susan be doing in Texas? As far as he knew, she'd never been to Texas in her life. You'd have to be *going* to Texas to go to Texas. It wasn't as if it was on the way to anywhere else, except Mexico. But—he thought about it—that was if you were going south. If you were driving from east to west, you might go *through* the state, and that would take you through West Texas.

"Call me when you find out anything, anything at all." Sharon was worried; finally a very real concern for her sister had broken through her busy social life. She added, "If you find out anything, you'll let me know, won't you?"

"Of course," he promised. "I'll have Susan call you herself, and we'll all laugh over the mix-up." He said the words, but in his gut he didn't believe them.

He replaced the receiver and went straight to the bookshelf and pulled out an atlas. Mendoza watched as he found first a map of Texas and then a map of the entire U.S. Brannigan ran a finger from North Carolina due west to Phoenix. His finger passed above Pecos, missing it by what looked like a couple of hundred miles, according to the graph.

Mendoza looked on. He said, "Allowing for the scarcity of highways through West Texas, she might have decided to go through Pecos."

"But once she got that far—and that's a long haul with two small children—what on earth would change her mind? What could have happened to make her change direction?"

"Something unexpected. One of the kids got sick? Car trouble?" Mendoza suggested.

"Either one is possible. But then, where is she? And why change her plans completely? If she was angry enough to drive all that way with two little kids, what happened to turn her around?"

"Guilt?" Mendoza offered. "For leaving in the first place?"

"Still, where is she?" Brannigan stared at him. "She's had plenty of time to get back, even allowing for side trips. Why isn't she here?"

Mendoza said, "All right. Let's follow this in another direction. Suppose she'd decided for some reason that her sister was not the one to be with while she was upset. Where would she go from Pecos, Texas? Who does she know near there?"

Brannigan looked down at the map and thought about it. "No one," he said. "As far as I know, not a soul." He looked up and stared intently at Mendoza.

"Are you sure?" Mendoza's dark eyes stared back at him.

Brannigan nodded. "There's something wrong, I'm telling you. I feel it in my gut."

"What? What's wrong?" Mendoza raised his voice for the first time. "What is it that you think has happened to her?"

"I don't know!"

Mendoza's eyes were tense, charged, as he brought up the frightening possibility and said it aloud. "Foul play?"

"No. Well, yes. Something to hold her there. Or somewhere. I don't know!" Brannigan jumped up and threw the atlas onto the sofa. He ran his fingers through his hair. "Don't ask me to explain it. I can't. I just know something has happened."

"Then what are you going to do?" Mendoza stared at him, challenging him. He knew how badly Brannigan needed to take action, needed to take steps to do something about his missing wife. He corrected himself—his missing *family.*

Brannigan's expression looked strained—haggard, even—and Mendoza knew what the man was going to say before he opened his mouth, before the first audible syllable escaped his throat.

"I'm going out there."

Susan fought as the beast pulled at her, tore at her clothing, wrenched her arm, and tore her heart out. She woke and found Cressman looming above her. He had wrenched Bryan from her arms and held him as a trump card above her head. Around her the rock crowded, wet and hard against her back, and the rain dripped and ran in rivulets along the gullies in the thirsty ground.

She had fallen asleep! She couldn't believe she'd let her guard down and given in to her tired body and exhausted spirit.

"Get up," Cressman told her. His tone made it clear that he was angry; it was undisguised. Susan pulled herself upright, the muscles in her back and knees stiff and painful. She clutched the baby to her for fear Cressman would wrench her away too. He forced Susan into his pickup truck, and then he put a hand on her face as if he would caress it, but he tightened his hold until his fingers dug into her flesh. Susan gasped at the pain, but he wouldn't relent. "I'm tired of you trying to get away from me." His eyes hardened. "You won't do it again."

Bryan reached for her, terrified. He cried, "Mommy!"

Cressman released her, slammed the door shut, and banged her knee. He got into the truck and jerked it into gear, and he said only one thing to her during the ride back. "I hope the kids don't get sick."

If his comment had been calculated to make her feel guilty, it had worked.

In the house, Cressman took the baby away from her and took both children to Maria for a warm bath. Then he ordered Susan to do the same. Her spirit beaten, she did as she was told. By the time she finished bathing and dressing, Chrissy was crying to be fed; Susan sat quietly in the rocking chair and fed Chrissy while Bryan ate breakfast at the little play table beside her in the bedroom that Cressman referred to as the nursery.

Maria came in and out several times during the morning, but Susan avoided making eye contact with her. When Maria left them alone, Susan found herself wondering what the woman knew and what she might be thinking. How had Cressman explained Susan's presence in the first place, and what had he said now that Susan had been forced to return? Did the woman suspect that she'd been brought to the ranch against her will? Susan wished for the first time that she had taken Spanish instead of French in high school. But, even as she thought it, she knew the odds were that she wouldn't have remembered enough to communicate with anyone anyway.

When Cressman came to the room later, he sat down near the rocking chair. Susan didn't speak to him; she continued to rock back and forth with Chrissy snuggled against her breast, sound asleep. She looked over at Bryan and saw him pick up his food and smash it between his fingers.

"Don't play with your food, Bryan. If you're finished eating, come over here and let me clean your hands." Bryan ambled over and leaned against the arm of the rocker. Susan stopped rocking, afraid that she'd rock on his toes. She pulled a baby wipe from the package and wiped his hands and face. She held his face and looked at him. He looked like a little miniature of his father. "All clean," she said, and she kissed him on the nose. Every last effort she could make would be to keep things as normal as possible for the children. She asked Bryan, "Do you want to play with the blocks now?" He nodded and rushed across the room to get the blocks.

"I want to talk to you," Cressman said. "I'm very upset over what you did."

"*You're* upset!" She couldn't believe her ears or his nerve.

"You took such a risk. I won't have you taking the children anywhere. You could have been hurt, all of you. You will not do that again. I told you it was too far to walk. And you need to face it, Susan, you're never going to leave here." A loud crash jolted them, and they jumped simultaneously. Bryan had dumped the box of blocks onto the floor.

"There are all kinds of dangers out there, Susan—snakes, wild javelinas, coyotes, gila monsters, and more." Susan thought of the "snake" she had encountered, but she didn't smile. She knew there were snakes out there that were real enough. Cressman changed his tactic. "I want you to come down to the barn with me. And I want Bryan to come too. Maria will stay with the baby."

"I don't think so. I don't want to go." Susan began rocking again, although the baby was sound asleep. Maybe the motion was for a comfort to her too.

"You know, that's the problem, Susan. You aren't even willing to try. The kids are adapting better than you are because you're making no effort. I want you to come with me to the barn. Bryan is coming, aren't you, Bryan?"

Bryan looked up from his blocks. He said, "I want to see my daddy."

Susan looked at Cressman to see what effect Bryan's words had on him, but he never so much as blinked. "Would you like to see the baby calf, Bryan? I think we should show him to your mommy. Maybe she'll like that."

Bryan jumped up and ran across the room in a hurry; he took hold of Susan's hand. "Come on, Mommy. I want to see the baby cow."

Chapter Eighteen

Never had a flight taken so long, and Kevin Brannigan had flown hundreds of times. The terminally endless flight related directly to the anxiety that plagued him. And when he was not feeling anxious, he was riddled with guilt. Had he neglected his family? Had he been so engrossed in his career that he didn't see Susan's unhappiness? He'd been attentive when he was home, but that left long stretches of time when she was alone with the children, often with him not coming home at the end of the day. Was that it? Was it the long hours unbroken by another adult to talk to?

He stared out the window of the plane at the billowed clouds and the blue stretching as far as he could see. Clear skies, always good for flying. He looked down at the minuscule farmhouses below and the even smaller cars and trucks on the roads. Any one person down there was a mere dot on the planet, but were their problems any smaller by comparison?

The captain's voice came over the PA, smooth and professional, announcing the landing and the temperature in the area—ninety-eight degrees. A rustle moved through the cabin like a wave as passengers got themselves ready, hoping to be quick in the line to deplane.

As the wheels touched ground, Brannigan imagined a collective sigh among the passengers. As amazing as flight was, and convenient, it was always a relief to be on the ground again. The plane taxied to a full stop, and the chatter among the passengers grew louder.

"Excuse me."

Brannigan turned toward the voice behind him. A woman seated alone asked, "I wondered if you would mind getting my bag down?" She had one arm in a sling, and she looked at him with clear green eyes. Her hair was a beige brown with random silver strands in it. She probably had twenty or more years on him, but she was aging gracefully.

He had noticed her, but in the same way he'd noticed the seat in front of his face, his thoughts projected ahead to what he would find in Pecos. But he could hardly refuse to help. "I'd be glad to," he said, and he opened the compartment above their seats.

"The black one there." She pointed. A couple of young guys pushed past and jostled them.

"Oh, I'm sorry," one of the guys called back.

The woman just smiled, and her smile was dazzling. She said, "They're so young, they're in a hurry to grasp life."

Brannigan replied sardonically, "That's being kind."

"Oh, thanks." She smiled again. She smoothed her dress, which was a soft green and white print that went perfectly with the green of her eyes. He was impatient to get away, and he turned his attention back to the bags and said, "Let me carry this for you."

"If you don't mind," she said.

"Not at all," was all he could think to say. He wanted to be out and moving.

"We are going the same direction," she said, and she bestowed another of those smiles on him.

"We are?" He looked puzzled.

"Yes," she said, and then at his confusion, she said, "out."

He laughed and ushered her ahead of him. They walked through the plane, up the Jetway, and down the concourse together. By the time they reached the main doors of the terminal, he'd learned she was coming to visit her daughter and grand-children, and she'd been told that he was there to pick up his wife. More than that, he didn't share.

Brannigan carried her bag to her daughter's car where it was pulled up to the curb and then watched as they hugged each other. The woman waved at Brannigan as they drove away.

He felt a pang of loneliness, and he thought of Susan. What would it be like to grow old with the woman you loved? To share all those years together, to watch her mature and then age? For a moment he was lost in the thought, but then he shook himself, mentally if not visibly, and went in search of the car-rental agency.

Susan slipped into the shower while Chrissy remained content to burble baby sounds in her bed and Bryan still slept. The hot water restored and refreshed tense muscles from a night of restless half sleep. Her mind had run in all directions except the one needed for rest; mostly she'd flayed herself with accusatory questions. Why hadn't she come up with some way to get her children away from this godforsaken ranch and the increasingly psychotic rancher? She worried as she dried off, just what was he capable of?

Susan pulled on a pair of white jean shorts and a cornflower-blue tank top and brushed her hair vigorously. She slipped her feet into her white sandals and tiptoed into the children's room. Chrissy, by that time, had pulled herself up onto her hands and knees but couldn't seem to move forward or back. "Hey, sweetie," Susan crooned softly. "What's wrong?" She picked the baby up and held her close. "You can't get into gear? You can't go?"

The baby looked at her, squinted her eyes, and laughed. Susan couldn't help but laugh too. She sat down in the rocker to feed the baby, rocking the chair gently and grateful for the one thing that some women overlooked about breastfeeding. In the fast-paced, modern world, the boon it offered was stopping everything and sitting quietly in the moment. For the length of time it took to feed her baby, there was nothing else that was more important to do.

Chrissy tugged at a lock of Susan's hair and played with it as she filled her tummy. Beside the rocker, Bryan woke and sat up. "Mommy?"

"Hi, buddy. Did you have a good rest?"

He nodded, still groggy with sleep, and pulled at his pajamas, which had become twisted as he slept. The bright blue background of his pajamas was filled with cars—red ones, yellow ones, and green ones. He was a walking advertisement for NASCAR. Kevin had selected the pajamas, so it must have been a guy thing.

"Are you hungry, buddy? Are you ready for some breakfast?"

"I want pancakes."

On the way back from the shower, Susan had caught the scent of Maria's cooking. "I think Maria is making tacos. Do you want a taco?"

Bryan scowled. "I don't want tacos. I want pancakes."

"But you love tacos," she reminded him.

"I want pancakes," Bryan stated emphatically. "I want Mickey pancakes."

"All right, then, let's go out to the kitchen." Susan reasoned away his stubborn demands by reminding herself that he was hardly in his usual element, far away from his normal life.

In the kitchen they found Maria cooking *papas con huevos*—potatoes and eggs—for tacos. Susan put Chrissy into the high chair and gave her slices of banana to toy with and, she hoped, eat, and then she made several attempts to explain to Maria that Bryan wanted pancakes. The problem was, they had a basic communication problem, and that thought reminded Susan of an old movie and the character stating, "What we have here is a failure to communicate."

Susan tried again, asking, "Where's Cressman?" She repeated the question a second time, as if the very act of restating the thought might close the gap of understanding.

Maria latched on to the one familiar word. "Señor Cressman?

Señor Cressman go." She said more, but since it was in the language Maria was most comfortable with, it was Susan's turn to look blank. She shrugged and began searching for a frying pan other than the one Maria was using. Once she found and assembled all the ingredients, she made pancake batter. She then poured one medium-size pool of batter into the middle of the pan and then added two smaller pools for Mickey Mouse's ears. She flipped the pancakes, and once they were done, she put them on a plate and searched in the fridge for fruit to use for Mickey's face. She found raisins and lined them up for Mickey's mouth and cut two slices of banana and used them for two big round eyes. Chrissy sat in the high chair happily fingering her banana, then smashed it and put her fingers into her mouth. When Susan placed the plate with Mickey Mouse pancakes in front of Bryan, he smiled and dug in.

The morning hours passed quickly. Susan helped Bryan build towers of blocks, and then the two of them gave pretend shrieks when Chrissy reached for the towers and knocked them down. Later, after lunch and to help them settle down, Susan read books to them.

While the children napped, Susan wandered restlessly through the house. The living room was cool but lifeless, although Maria kept it, as well as everything else, meticulous. The living room represented no cleaning challenge, since Susan had yet to see anyone ever use it, not even once. The picture of Cressman's wife, which she'd seen before, caught her interest, and she crossed the room to take a closer look. The frame felt cold when Susan picked it up, no doubt due to the air-conditioning, but it chilled Susan to think about the woman who'd lived here. Had she been happy on the ranch? Had she loved John Cressman? Surely she had at some point and maybe until the day she died, leaving him alone in the isolation.

Susan replaced the picture, putting it in the exact place it had been, even though there was no dust to show displacement. She looked at the photo one last time. Something nagged at

Susan. There was something familiar about Cressman's wife, but it eluded her.

She wandered from the living room and then on down the hall. She reached the closed doors of the rooms at the far end of the hall, and, on impulse, she opened the door just past the bathroom. The room was a bedroom, spare and masculine, with one of Cressman's shirts hung over a chair. She closed the door and went on. A painting hung on the wall. It pictured a mustang being broken, the rider hanging on with everything he could muster, the muscles in his arms like ropes in tension. The painting looked amateurish but better than a beginner might do.

Susan moved on and opened the next door and found another bedroom. This one was decidedly feminine, with a lime-green-and-brown floral print on the comforter and its flounces. The shams looked faded, as if they'd been washed often, and the colors looked like something popular in past decades. Susan turned and looked at the wall beside her, and she gasped. The entire wall had been covered with pictures of John Cressman's wife, large formal portraits, small snapshots, young, old—the room was a shrine.

Susan felt suddenly uncomfortable being there, seeing the commemoration, uncomfortable with the pain of the man who'd done this, who'd set this up. But there was something . . . Susan bent closer and focused on one particular picture of Cressman's wife, one where she appeared to be in her twenties and wore a white blouse and had her hair tied back with a ribbon. Susan stared; she hadn't realized just how much she resembled Cressman's dead wife. The woman was blond, blue-eyed; her hair hung down to her shoulders and had been lightened by the sun. She looked out on the world with a fresh, eager anticipation, her lips turned up in a wide smile.

So similar. The thought was not a comfortable one. Cressman must have seen the resemblance from the beginning. He'd seen it the moment he laid eyes on Susan out on the dusty road. Susan saw it now, and it unnerved her.

Chapter Nineteen

By the time he arrived in the dusty West Texas town, Kevin Brannigan felt a temporary loss as to what his next step should be. He searched for a rental agency and chose a car, then went in search of a motel. It didn't take long to register and stow his suitcase in his room. The motel manager gave him directions to the Western Union office, and he found it located within a small grocery store on the west side of the city. Brannigan felt an unexpected sense of dread as he reached for the door. That puzzled him and stopped him briefly. By all logic, he should be experiencing a surge of optimism because he was at last taking action.

Lizzie Gray stood behind the counter in the store, working on the books with the usual sense of irritation that activity brought out in her. She looked up when the door opened. A man entered, and Lizzie lost interest in the books. It was not every day that an unfamiliar face, and a strikingly handsome one at that, came through her door. His shirt matched the blue gray of his eyes—no easy feat, because it was a beautiful but uncommon shade—and Lizzie was neither too old nor too bereft of hormones to notice. He had a lean, tight physical build that she approved of, albeit in silence.

"Can I help you?" Lizzie asked.

The woman's West Texas twang was obvious to Brannigan if not to her.

"I hope so. I'm looking for someone, and I have reason to believe she was here about five days ago. Maybe six."

"What does she look like?"

"Slim, blond hair, blue eyes. You'd remember her," he said as he pulled a photo of Susan from his pocket.

Lizzie took the picture from him and studied it. "I see what you mean. She's a pretty thing."

"You saw her?" Brannigan asked.

"No, I'm afraid not."

"But you said—" He looked puzzled.

"I said that she's someone I would remember if I had seen her. But I haven't."

"Are you absolutely certain?" He hesitated. "Please, it's very important, ma'am. She would have had two small children with her."

Lizzie looked at the picture again and then gave it back to him. "I'm sorry," she said, and her tone was genuine. Her voice softened. "I wish I could help you, but as near as I can tell, I've never seen her before."

Stunned, Brannigan stood for a moment as if he'd been hit in the midsection. He had expected—no, he had been certain—he would receive an affirmative reply, that all he'd have to do was come in and ask. But then the obvious hit him, and he smiled in relief. "There must have been someone else working that day."

She shook her head. "Nope. No one works here but me."

"No one?" Brannigan studied the woman, unsure whether he should believe her. Her gray hair was done up neatly, her face an impassive mask. She looked honest, and she would have no reason to bend the truth.

"This isn't Dallas or Houston. We barely keep busy enough for me." At that, she smiled.

"No one else handles the telegrams?" He indicated the separate cubicle in a corner of the store marked WESTERN UNION. "What about when you're sick or on vacation? There must be someone who fills in for you."

"There is. It's Jake over at the drugstore. Only I haven't been sick in six months, and I haven't had a vacation in twice that long."

"What about your lunch hour? Does he fill in for you then?"

"Humph. Lunch hour? No. I eat here. I pack a lunch from home, or I call over to the café and have someone bring me something."

"I see," Brannigan said, but in fact he didn't. How could it be possible that she had never laid eyes on Susan?

"Is there another Western Union office in town?"

Lizzie laughed. "Are you kidding? I told you, we barely have enough work for me to do. Sorry."

Brannigan started for the door. "Thanks."

The man's disappointment was evident in the slump of his shoulders. Lizzie, always a sucker for the downtrodden, stopped him. She said, "Do you have the telegram with you?"

He turned back. "What?"

"Do you have the telegram? I could see if it came from this office and check my paperwork. I don't know if that will help, but we could try."

"I don't have it," he told her.

"Oh." Lizzie didn't know what else she could do for him, and she was about to say so, when he spoke up.

"I can get it. It'll take me a while, but I'll be back. In the meantime, if you remember anything, will you call me? I'm staying at the Mountain View Motel. My name's Brannigan. Kevin Brannigan."

When he left the telegram office, Brannigan drove to the motel and called Sharon. He arranged for her to send the telegram by overnight mail. Dinner in the motel restaurant and a drive through the city's streets killed the evening hours but did nothing to ease his anxious mind.

Brannigan called Mendoza long distance and told him about the unexpected response at the telegram office. Although it was left unsaid by Mendoza, Brannigan knew that he thought it had been a futile trip to begin with. He stretched out on the bed and lay awake until the morning hours, unable to sleep.

When sleep finally came, it was filled with uneasy dreams of the worst kind, where you run and run and can never reach whatever it is you're trying to get. He was in a long tunnel, and he started out walking and searching for something—at that point he didn't know what. Bizarre creatures appeared at the entrances to other tunnels, offshoots of the main tunnel. The creatures were misshapen or ill-formed, but he recognized them as enemies without understanding how he knew that fact. Even in his dream he realized that it was all cloak-and-dagger-ish, but he gave it little thought because he knew he was desperate to find something or someone. And somehow the fact was conveyed to him that time was running out.

He began to run until, finally, there in the tunnel ahead of him he saw a figure—hazy at first and with a mist that obscured her—but he recognized the figure of a woman. When the haze cleared, he saw that it was Susan. A gauzy length of white fabric was wrapped around her body and trailed after her. Her long blond hair reflected in lights in the tunnel, and both her hair and the gauzy cloth blew, undulating with a breeze, and she reached out her hand for him to come.

Brannigan woke in a panic and turned on the lights in the room: 5:00 A.M. He leaned back in the bed, but he couldn't settle down. The bed was not very comfortable, and neither were the pillows; what he did not want to admit, even to himself, was how disturbed he was by the dream. Like so many dreams, it had felt real; he had been there, and Susan had eluded him. That was what disturbed him and felt like a portent of things to come. He sat up and punched the pillows, beating them into submission, and then he lay back with such force that he squashed them again. Who was he angry at? It was just a dream after all. But it didn't take a Freudian expert to understand what the dream meant.

Chapter Twenty

Susan inhaled the dusty, dry hay smell and the musky scent of horses, and it occurred to her that the ranch would have been a wonderful place for a vacation under normal circumstances. She watched as Bryan rolled around in the hay until it stuck all over his hair and clothes and gave him the unmistakable look of a miniature scarecrow sidetracked from Oz. He jumped onto Susan's lap in a rush and knocked her back onto the mound of hay. His giggles drew a smile from her.

"You're a silly-willy," she told Bryan.

"I'm a hay man." He laughed.

"What is a hay man?"

"A man who sells hay," he said matter-of-factly.

"Of course." She smiled. "I should have known."

Bryan ran across the barn and returned with one of the puppies. He asked eagerly, "Do you like this one, Mommy?"

Susan took the puppy and looked at the tiny animal blinking sleepily at her. The puppy was all warm velvet and freckled tummy and had the unmistakable scent of the very young. "I like it very much," she said, holding the puppy's softness against her cheek, his fur a creamy mocha color.

"May I take him home with me?"

Susan hesitated. *Home.* What a pleasant picture that was. Images of their home came to her, and she wished the proverbial wish of everyone who'd ever found themselves in some situation too difficult to handle; she wished she could turn back the clock to that fateful moment when she and Kevin had argued.

"May I, Mommy? May I?" Bryan's enthusiasm for the dog was a down-to-earth situation that relieved the tension and anxiety she'd been feeling. But Susan didn't want to make a promise that might not be in her ability to keep. She said, "Well, first of all, this puppy is not a he; it's a she." Susan nuzzled her nose against the puppy's fur. "This puppy is a little girl dog."

Bryan looked at the dog and appeared to be taking in this new information, but he took the puppy and set her on his lap and ran a hand down her back. "May I have a puppy? May I?"

Susan smiled at him and gave him the answer parents often resorted to. "We'll see, Bryan." He was still too young to recognize that the answer meant maybe yes but most likely no—in other words, no commitment.

When Cressman returned to the barn half an hour later, he found the two of them snuggled on the hay together. Both Bryan and the puppy had been lulled into sleep on Susan's lap.

Susan did not fall asleep; she feared she might never sleep again. She was afraid. She'd never known fear like this in her life. What if she couldn't escape from this ranch?

Brannigan waited for the mail delivery and brooded. It was all he could do. He thought about the four years since the day he and Susan got married. The first year they'd been happier than he had believed possible, and, for that matter, the rest of the years had been happy too. More hectic once the children were born, but still happy. What had gone wrong? What caused her to pack up and drive halfway across the country with the children? Why had she left her home? Had she been that miserable? Had that one argument been the pivotal point, the deciding factor? Had it been the reason she'd left him, the final straw?

Just weeks ago they'd celebrated Bryan's third birthday, and everything had been perfect. It had rained all day, but the weather didn't dampen their fun. Bryan had been delighted with his presents, and the entire evening had been enjoyable. Kevin remembered watching Susan explain the piecing-together of a toy to Bryan as they sat in the middle of the floor and worked on it. The baby lay on her red and white quilt beside them, and she'd been content with gripping her newly discovered toes. Susan's long hair swung forward as she and Bryan worked together. Her hair had such a silky texture to it that it always amazed him when he touched it. And she wore it long and in a loose curl, nearly to the middle of her back; like a lot of men, he liked long hair on a woman. He remembered looking at his family and feeling lucky. At that moment she'd looked up and discovered him watching her.

"What?" she'd questioned, puzzled and trying to interpret his look.

He'd given her a lazy grin and said, "I'll tell you later."

Now here he sat, about a thousand miles away from that life, and the greatest fear of his life was that he might not get it back. He had to hold out hope; he had to. But first he had to find Susan. If he could find her, maybe he could make it right.

The ring of the phone jarred him from his thoughts; the motel office staff—aka the bent but friendly elderly man who ran the front desk—called to tell him that a letter had come for him. Brannigan rushed to the motel office to get it and then on to the store with the telegram office.

Lizzie had given some thought to writing a few letters; the store was quiet, the only noise the scratchy whine of the cicadas in the tree outside. When she saw Kevin Brannigan step from the car outside the door, her interest was piqued. Maybe the afternoon wouldn't be so boring after all. She noticed again his trim good looks and what people referred to as his military bearing. That phrase had always intrigued her. Wasn't it just a euphemism for good posture? Did that imply that anyone with a straight back, anyone who held himself or herself well, had a military bearing?

Brannigan came through the door and said, "Hi. Remember me?"

She smiled. *Forget him? As if.* "Did you get the telegram?"

"I did." He was almost boyish in his enthusiasm, a marked difference from his reserve of the day before. He gave her the telegram and, without the distraction of additional small talk, she studied it carefully. "Yes, it's from this office all right. And as a matter of fact, I did take it. 'Course, like I told you yesterday, there hasn't been anybody working here but me. So"—she paused for effect—"if a telegram's from here, I took it, and I sent it."

"But you said you didn't remember Susan. The woman who gave it to you."

"No, I didn't say that." Lizzie eyed him warily. "What I said was that I hadn't seen the girl in your picture. She didn't send the telegram. Someone else sent it."

"Someone else?" Kevin looked confused, as if he struggled to digest the information.

"You aren't going to go nuts on me, are you?"

"What do you mean? What are you talking about?"

"It was a man." Lizzie watched him carefully.

"A man?" A new tension filled the air. The hush of the afternoon grew long. Brannigan fought with the unexpected twist, and it became obvious that it was one possibility he hadn't considered. Also abundantly clear, at least to observers of human nature like Lizzie, was that the information hit him hard.

"He was an older man," Lizzie supplied unasked, hoping that would compensate for the fact that it had been a man.

"Older?" Brannigan was having difficulty getting past the first fact.

"About fifty, white hair—kind of silver," Lizzie offered. "He's well-dressed, drives a flashy car. Maybe a Cadillac."

"You know him?"

"No, but I've seen him. Not in here so much but around town."

"He's from here?" Brannigan pushed his fingers through his hair.

"Must be. I've seen him at the café. The Silver Stone. It's down the street on the right. You can ask there."

"Does he go there often?"

Lizzie thought about it. What was often? Frequency was a matter of opinion, meaning different things to different people. "Not real often but more than a couple of times. He may live on the outskirts of town, maybe on a ranch around here, or maybe he just travels through here occasionally. Ask for Ginger down at the café. She's a waitress there. She knows everything that goes on around here."

Brannigan thanked her and started toward the door. Before he opened it, he turned back and looked at Lizzie. "You're absolutely sure?" he asked. "About this man being the one who sent the telegram?"

Lizzie nodded. "I'm sure."

The Silver Stone Café occupied an old rock building at the end of the street. The exterior walls of the building were in dire need of sandblasting to clean the place up. Inside, the place had been decorated with gingham curtains, old farm implements, and rough-hewn wooden tables, the epitome of western decor. Brannigan crossed to a table in a corner and read the menu that had been painted directly onto the wall. As he did, he looked around the place for a middle-aged, silver-haired man, but he saw no one who matched that description. Two older women sat at a table near the door and laughed over some tidbit of shared gossip. Their expressions grew as conspiratorial as those of two naughty children. The only other customer was a woman in her mid-thirties with a hard edge to her face and tired dark eyes that she kept turning in his direction.

A tall, thin woman with orange hair came from the back carrying two plates. She set them in front of the two giggling ladies, and then she brought a glass of water to Brannigan's table. "Hi," she said. "What can I get you?"

"Are you Ginger?" he asked.

"Sure am. Who's asking?"

"My name's Kevin Brannigan. I was over at the store talking to the proprietor there. She said you might be able to help me with some information."

"I'll try." She smiled. "But let's put your order in first before José thinks it's time for a break."

"What do you recommend?"

"The Mexican plate."

"I'll have that."

"You're easy to please." She smiled again. "How 'bout to drink? Beer?"

"No, just water." He had steered clear of alcohol during the past few days. He wanted a clear head.

"Be right back," she told him.

Kevin leaned back in the uncomfortable chair. He saw that the woman who was seated by herself was still watching him. She looked lonely, and for some reason he thought of Susan. Was she lonely for him at all? Was she all right? He didn't know what to think.

Ginger returned, and this time she brought a glass of iced tea and sat down across from him.

"What can I help you with?"

"I'm looking for someone," Brannigan began, pulling the picture from his pocket.

Ginger took it and looked at it. "Pretty girl," she said, "but I don't think I've ever seen her."

"She sent a telegram from here, to her sister. No one's heard from her since. I'm trying to trace her. The woman at the Western Union office—"

"Lizzie."

"Yes, Lizzie. Lizzie said the telegram was sent from her office, but a man sent it. She didn't know who he was, but she said she's seen him in here before."

"What does this fella look like?"

"Silver hair, fiftyish, and she thinks he's a rancher or

someone who travels through here on occasion. And he might drive a Cadillac or something like that."

"White?"

"What?"

"A white Cadillac?"

"She didn't say."

"Let me call her. I'll be right back."

Brannigan watched her walk away. Was everyone in town this friendly? He wondered about this mystery man, the Cadillac owner. What was he to Susan? Or she to him?

"Want some company?"

Brannigan looked up. The woman who'd looked so lonely now stood beside his chair. Her thin body was encased in tight jeans, and her hair hung straight till it settled on her collarbone. She leaned one thin hip forward, slanted toward him, and looked at him without blinking. He hadn't answered her, but she didn't wait. "I haven't seen you before." She blew smoke from her cigarette, and her eyes squinted to look through the haze.

"No, I'm just passing through."

"It figures. Anyone who looks as good as you can't be from around here."

"I'm looking for my wife." There, that brought it out into the open.

"Why? She lost?" The woman smiled and took another long pull on her cigarette.

Brannigan was surprised that the restaurant was not smoke-free. Maybe the owner didn't want to get on the bad side of his customers, especially the regulars. "Sort of," he told the woman.

"Well"—she leaned in close—"if you get tired of looking for her, you let me know. All right?"

"Thanks." Lame, but it was all he could think to say.

Ginger returned, gave the woman a pointed look that said *take off,* and then she sat back down across from Brannigan. She said, "John."

Brannigan's pulse jumped. "John?"

"I don't know his last name. He doesn't come in often. I think we're a little too down-home for him."

"Do you know where he lives?"

"No, but I got the feeling he owns a ranch around here. He does drive a white Cadillac."

"I need to find him."

Ginger studied his face carefully and wondered if this was something she should stay out of. She asked, "Who's the girl in the picture?"

"My wife." He said it in a simple, direct tone, but he guessed she would realize there was much more to the story. And there was so much more.

"Wait here," she said, and she went back to the phone. He watched from across the room as she punched in numbers and then spoke into the phone. When she came back this time, she told him, "I spoke to Jake over at the drugstore. He knows everybody for miles around. He says the guy lives out near Fleming. That's a little spot in the road west of here. You go southwest on twenty until it connects with ten, then you take ten west just like you were going to Van Horn, but before that you'll see a sign for Fleming. It's a few miles off the highway."

Brannigan thanked her and headed out the door, having eaten no more than a few bites of his Mexican plate. Fleming. What would he find there? Would this stop turn out any better than the others? Would it be another place that provided no clues in this otherwise fruitless search? He was sorry he'd ever volunteered for that last mission. He had to find Susan; he couldn't give up. He wouldn't give up.

Chapter Twenty-one

The road to Fleming failed to impress Brannigan. The land was dry and dusty, any greenery sparse and stunted. In fact, shrubs were nonexistent other than the brush that stretched to the foothills of the mountains. Driving down the road, Brannigan wondered again where this would take him—not where in the literal, physical direction, but into what new and unexplored emotional territory would he be drawn? Had Susan left him for this silver-haired man? And, if so, when had they met? *How* had they met? His thoughts, just like the facts, would not click. They failed to fall into a recognizable, familiar pattern. Brannigan knew one thing for certain: Susan had never mentioned this man to him. Ever. He would have remembered.

A small town appeared on the horizon, and Brannigan slowed. When he reached the center of the small cluster of buildings that made up the town, he pulled into the gas station. He climbed out of the car, determined to find Susan, although he could think of no earthly reason Susan would be out here in the middle of nowhere, where, as far as he knew, she didn't know a soul.

A middle-aged man came through the door, wiping his hands on a greasy rag. Judging from the grease on his chin, the man was wiping away his lunch, not the usual sort of grease found in gas stations. The man smiled broadly and explained unnecessarily, "Sorry, I was eating my lunch. What can I do for you?"

A brief flash of instinct made Brannigan pause, and he glanced down at the fuel indicator. "How about a fill-up?" he asked.

"Sure thing." The man pushed the nozzle into place and asked, "Check under the hood?"

Kevin told him yes, knowing that everything under the hood would check out fine. He stepped out of the car and leaned against it in an easygoing, no-hurry manner.

"Sure is hot." Opening gambit—*don't rush it,* he told himself.

"It's hot here every day."

"I guess you get used to it."

"If it don't kill you first." The man chuckled at his own joke. "Where you from?"

"California, originally," Brannigan answered honestly.

"Oh." The lone syllable made a statement. Brannigan was unsure what it meant, but he had encountered it before from non-Californians. Did they think all Californians were alike? And were . . . what? Hedonists? Flakes?

The hood dropped into place. "Everything's fine under the hood." The owl-shaped face began to concentrate on the dusty windshield.

"Do you get many people passing through here?" Brannigan asked with caution.

"Hardly any. This ain't exactly the road to Rome." He chuckled again.

"Or even New York," Kevin said.

"That's right." The man chuckled.

"Then you'd remember someone new who happened to come by."

The large hand polishing the glass stopped, an almost imperceptible hesitation, before he resumed the motion. "I guess so."

Brannigan pulled the snapshot from his pocket. "Have you seen her?"

Big brown eyes peered at Brannigan through thick glasses and then glanced at the picture. "No, I don't think so. She sure is pretty, though. Is she yours?"

Brannigan thought about that. He hoped she still was.

The man pulled the pump handle out and hung it up. "That'll be twenty-four fifty."

Brannigan reached for his billfold and extended thirty dollars before he said, "Keep the change."

"Thanks." The man pocketed the bills and turned away.

"You're sure about the picture?" Brannigan asked.

The man looked him up and down. "Are you a detective?"

"No." Where had that come from, and why would the man jump to that conclusion?

"What's this woman to you?" The dark eyes blinked at him.

"She's my wife," Kevin said simply.

Shaggy eyebrows rose a fraction. "Oh. No. I can't help you. Sorry." He made a hasty retreat back to the office and, presumably, his lunch.

Brannigan got back into the car and started the engine. Before he pulled away, he could see through the window that the man had gone straight to the telephone. *Now, that's odd.* Why would the man rush straight to the phone while his lunch was waiting for him? Brannigan also wondered why he hadn't asked the man about the rancher while he had the chance. He didn't know for sure, but something wily in the guy's expression had alerted him to keep what little he knew from this man. And his instincts had served him well many times before.

For now, he would concentrate on the business at hand. Or businesses. Those lining either side of the street. He guessed that the café and the grocery store were the most likely stops for Susan to make. He decided to try the café first.

The Bluebonnet Café was a misnomer. There were no bluebonnets anywhere around that he could see. Business was slow at the café—only two customers—but then, for all he knew, this could be their rush hour. The waitress brought a menu along with a cheery greeting, and he ordered a plate of enchiladas. At this rate he'd become an expert on Tex-Mex cuisine before the trip ended.

The waitress returned and stayed to chat, maybe out of boredom or curiosity. A middle-aged woman on the plump side, her name tag read: LINDA. She asked him, "Are you passing through?"

"Yes," he told her. "I'm looking for someone." He pulled the picture from his pocket again in a now-automatic gesture and showed it to her.

She took a long look. "Yeah, I saw her. She's awfully pretty. Is she your wife or your girlfriend or something?"

"She's my wife." Brannigan's calm exterior belied the rapid beat of his pulse. "You've seen her, then? She would have had two children with her."

"Well, I don't have the best memory in the world, but . . ." Her eyes were fixed on some point past Brannigan's head. He turned to see the owl-faced man from the gas station.

"Could I talk to you, Linda?" the man said.

"Sure thing," Linda told him. "Be right there."

"Now," Owl-face insisted.

"Sure, Ed." To Brannigan, she said, "I'll be right back." She followed the man out the door and was gone for several minutes. When they returned, she asked, "How are those enchiladas?"

"They're fine." Brannigan replied.

"Now, where were we?" she asked.

"You were telling me about the picture. You said you saw her. Do you remember where?"

"Let me take a look at the picture again. My memory's not the best."

Brannigan gave her the picture, feeling close to his first solid clue to Susan's disappearance. Finally.

"No, I'm sorry, but I'm just not sure."

He stared at her. "You said you had seen her."

"I thought I had, but, you know, now that I've taken a good look at it, I'm just not sure." She stared at the picture, her eyes troubled and edged with something else. What was it? He thought about it for a moment, and then it came to him. Sadness. Her eyes were edged with genuine sorrow. Why, he wondered.

"This is very important." His eyes pleaded if his voice didn't. "She's my wife, and we have two small children. They're missing, and I've got to find them."

"I'm sorry," she told him. "I don't know anything that will help you."

"Are you sure?" He couldn't give up, couldn't let it go.

She nodded. "I'm sorry," she said again, and she plucked at the edge of her well-worn apron. Her glance flicked away again and again. Brannigan turned and saw the man from the gas station again sitting in the corner booth. "Do you know that man in the booth back there?"

"Sure," she said. "That's my husband, Ed."

Brannigan finished his meal, then stepped up to the register to pay for it. The waitress walked toward the front to take the money. Her eyes were large and expressive, and he felt there was something unfinished between them, as if she wanted to say more but couldn't. Or wouldn't. Which was it? He had no way of knowing, and if she wouldn't talk to him, there was no way he could find out.

Outside, he scanned the perimeter of the town. It was situated in the middle of nowhere. What had brought Susan to this town? If she had come here at all. Perhaps he had come this far for nothing.

The grocery store could fit into half the space of the restaurant, but it held much more—produce, shipping carts, rows of canned and boxed food, and the checkout counter. Unlike the megamarkets of the big cities, it had the crowded, overstocked look of the old corner grocery stores of years ago.

A large woman stood behind the register and fanned her face with a copy of *Woman's Day*. She greeted Brannigan the moment he walked in the door. "How're you doing?"

"Fine," he told her, and he wasted no time but pulled the picture out of his pocket right away. "I'm looking for someone," he told her. "I thought you might have seen her."

The woman stopped fanning herself and called out to someone unseen at the rear of the store. "Fred, check that air conditioner again. It's getting worse up here." She took the picture and apologized to Brannigan. "I'm sorry, I have to get on him all the time. The air conditioner's not working like it should, and he don't want to do anything about it. He's got a real head-in-the-sand attitude about repairs. He thinks if you ignore it, maybe it'll go away. I wish all problems in life were that easy to fix." She looked at the photo, even studied it carefully. "No, I can't say as I've ever seen her. I sure don't think so, and I think I would remember, 'cause we don't get too many visitors here." She looked at Brannigan. "You're the first one we've seen in a week."

"This is very important," he urged.

"Okay, then, I'll bite. Who is she, and why are you so desperate to find her?"

"She's my wife, and she's missing. I have reason to believe she came here."

The woman looked at the picture again and gave it careful consideration. "I'm sorry, but I don't remember ever seeing her." She gave the picture back to Brannigan.

"She would have had two small children with her," he added.

She shook her head in sympathy, but her expression held a tinge of something else. Curiosity? Curiosity barely restrained by good manners evidently made it impossible for her to ask why he found it necessary to search for his family.

At the door he turned toward her and asked, "Do you know a rancher around here named John something? He drives a Cadillac—a white one, I think."

"Sure. That would be John Cressman. He lives out west of town a few miles." Her curiosity was definitely piqued, and she waited for more, but nothing was forthcoming.

In the car, minutes later, the hastily drawn directions on the seat beside him, Brannigan had to think just what he would say when he faced the rancher. *Excuse me, but did you send a telegram for my wife recently?* The entire story sounded pretty bizarre.

Chapter Twenty-two

Susan sat on the floor with both children on her lap; she often sat on the floor with them getting down to the level where they spent most of their time. She leaned against the bed that Bryan slept in; she refused to call it Bryan's bed, because Bryan's bed was at home. Their home. She thought of their home now, and she could picture it clearly, just as she'd left it. Never had she longed for it more than she did at that moment. To sit at the table with Kevin and Bryan with Chrissy in her high chair and all of them talking together about anything and nothing would be all that she could ask for.

Susan read *Goodnight, Moon* for the second time. Bryan had chosen it, and that was no surprise. It had been his favorite book for months. Susan read while Chrissy squirmed on her lap. Reading together was one of their favorite things to do, and it always helped to settle them. Right now she wondered if it did more for her than it did for the children. She was the one who needed settling. She sought inner quiet and the strength to help her protect her children, but her thoughts were as scattered and restless as Chrissy's small body. Susan felt incapable of achieving calm, either inner or outward.

Cressman appeared in the doorway and startled her, which did nothing to quiet her mood. "Come with me, and don't ask questions." He told Bryan, "Come on, son."

Susan looked at him and considered the unexpected request. "Where are we going?" she asked.

"I said no questions. Manuel is going take you out to see a part of the ranch you've never seen."

"Why?" she asked, resisting stubbornly.

"What?" Cressman hadn't heard her; in fact, he appeared distracted, focused on something else, and whatever it was, it disturbed him.

"You're not even going? Why are we going?"

"I thought you'd like to see it. Bryan wants to go, don't you, Bryan?"

Before Bryan could answer, Susan jumped in and said, "No, I don't think so." It irritated her the way Cressman tried to manipulate her by using Bryan every time he wanted her to do something.

"You will go." He grabbed her arm, and she flinched as if he'd struck her. He pulled her off the floor. "Don't question everything I tell you. Just do it. And bring the diaper bag. You may need it."

Susan watched as he led Bryan out the door. This was so wrong. Bryan thought of John as a friend and didn't hesitate to go with him. He would follow John anywhere, and that worried her more than anything else. Where was Cressman taking them now? Or sending them? And why?

The truck, parked near the rear of the house, had the motor running and the AC blowing. Cressman ushered Susan and the children into the front seat beside Manuel, one of the ranch hands, and then spoke to the man in Spanish. Did none of his employees speak English, as he'd told her?

Cressman put a hand on her knee; the touch had a proprietary air about it. Susan pulled away.

Surprisingly, he didn't react; he just said, "Enjoy yourself. You'll like it out there." A brief hesitation followed, as if he would say more, but then he slammed the door shut, and Manuel jerked the pickup into gear and drove off. He turned off the drive onto a dirt road, but he didn't speak at all.

"What's up?" Susan asked him. "What's going on?" The

man shrugged but said nothing. The man's face, weathered from too many years of working in the dry, hot air, revealed nothing. His dark eyes held a permanent squint from staring into the sun. What kind of men were these? These men who came here to this godforsaken stretch of earth at the back of the beyond and worked day after day in the unrelenting sun? What did they know about her? Did they know she was being held against her will? Did they simply do their jobs and ask no questions? Unlikely to find the answers, Susan turned her attention to the ranch land around her.

The countryside did not change. The land stretched far into the distance toward the mountains, and the only shade the land offered was from a few random mesquite trees and the low brush that grew everywhere.

Horses and cattle moved across the range; Susan pointed them out to Bryan, but they were not new to him anymore. He made daily trips to the barn to see the calf. And there were horses in the barn as well as the much-loved puppies. Bryan had become blasé about the farm animals, taking them as much for granted now as he had his toys back home.

Manuel turned the truck off the road and, heading south, followed a line of mesquites. The trees skirted a shallow ravine, a creek bed that was dry and dusty but likely had underground water. Manuel continued driving. The view did not change, and conversation remained nonexistent.

Bryan leaned against Susan's shoulder and asked her, "Where are we going, Mommy?" She'd buckled him into the center belt, and he didn't like to be restrained. The baby sat in her seat on Susan's lap and burbled at them.

She put her arm around his small shoulders and forced a smile to her face. "We're going to see some other part of the ranch."

"I want to see the puppies. I want to go to the barn."

"We'll see the puppies when we get back," she explained.

Bryan stomped his foot. "I want to see the puppies now!"

Susan looked at him, surprised. Her genial three-year-old had been replaced by a tiny tyrant. What had caused that? In a calm voice she said, "Sit still, buddy. We'll see the puppies soon. I promise."

Bryan acquiesced, understanding already in his young years that if she promised something, it would happen.

A ridge jutted out in front of them; Manuel turned the wheel and circled around it. Tucked against a slope in the land sat a small wooden structure, a cabin. Why anyone would build a cabin out in these godforsaken parts, she couldn't imagine.

Manuel pulled up in front of the cabin and turned the engine off. "Come on," he said. To Susan's amazement his words were in English.

"You speak English?" she asked.

"No. No. *Poco.*" He held two fingers up with a very small space between them. "Little."

"Can you help me?" she asked in desperation.

"No. *No hablo.*"

She stared at him in frustration and then looked at the cabin. *This* was what Cressman wanted her to see? It looked like little more than a shack. She sat unmoving till Manuel circled the truck and opened the door, prompting her to get out.

The cabin had been sparsely furnished with a narrow bed and a small cook stove, although she couldn't imagine the lonely soul desperate enough to live in this place. Near the front window a table and a couple of chairs stood, rickety and uninviting. Bryan roamed the one room with the intention of exploring, but even Bryan, with the insatiable curiosity of a three-year-old, was astute enough to see that there was little of interest in the cabin. He wandered toward the door.

Manuel got busy and pulled the table out the door onto the porch. He pulled the chairs out next, and then he retrieved a basket from the rear of the pickup. Susan watched as he emptied the contents of the basket onto the table. Bread, cheese, pickles, sliced ham, and a cooler filled with lemonade—as fresh and tasty a picnic lunch as she'd ever seen, all for their lunch. Had John thought of all this, and if so, why? Did he plan to join them out here in the back country?

The gate to the Cressman ranch, planted in natural rock, stood open, a cattle guard installed across the entrance to keep stray cattle from wandering off the ranch. Brannigan turned into the gate and followed the unpaved drive; his gut tightened as he approached the house. It had come to this, Brannigan thought, but would this man, this . . . cowboy, admit to sending the telegram for Susan? No one appeared when he stopped in front of the house, nor did anyone come out when he slammed the car door and adjusted his sunglasses. Far-off ranch hands miniaturized by distance moved cattle across the land. The only sound near at hand was the barking of a dog. No one appeared, no one curious about the approach of a stranger. Brannigan had seen no fences since the gate. He knocked on the front door and waited; a small, dark-skinned woman opened the door. "I'd like to see Mr. Cressman," he told her.

The woman stared at him with large dark eyes, so dark they appeared black, but she made no effort to move or speak. Brannigan wondered if she understood him. Her eyes, set in a small face, watched him warily. He wasted no time but pulled the picture from his pocket.

"I'm looking for someone," he said. "Have you seen this woman?" He held the picture out directly in her line of vision, and the dark eyes focused on the picture. Was there the smallest, almost imperceptible change in her expression? Eyelids twitching? Anything?

The door opened wide, and a man towered over the woman. He said, "*Gracias,* Maria."

Dark eyes flashed upward toward his, focused briefly, but then she turned away.

"Can I help you?"

"I'm looking for someone." Brannigan watched the man's

expression for any sign of recognition as he extended the snap-shot in what by now had become a familiar ritual. The man's eyes pierced Brannigan's, then dipped down toward the picture, but they returned to Brannigan's face immediately.

"We don't get too many people passing by. Too far from town."

"You haven't seen her, then?"

"No." Then, seemingly as an afterthought, he added, "Sorry."

"You're certain?"

"Absolutely."

Brannigan hesitated. "I received some information that led me to believe you might have seen her."

"No, I'm sorry. Whoever gave you that information was mistaken." His tone was dismissive; the rancher had nothing else to say.

Where was that famous Texas hospitality Brannigan had always heard about? Perspiration trickled down his hairline, behind his ears, and down his back. The cool air inside the door was only one reason to want in. "Could I trouble you for a glass of water?"

Cressman hesitated, appeared to evaluate the situation, and said, "Sure. Come on in." Brannigan followed the rancher into a spacious living room decorated with heavy wood furniture covered with bright cushions. In spite of the color of the cushions, the room looked lifeless and stale, as though it saw little use.

"Have a seat. I'll get your water."

Once the rancher left the room, Brannigan paced. The request for water had been a stalling tactic. He needed time to figure out what to do next. He wished he had more information about the man, the ranch, and whether he really was the one who'd sent the telegram. A hush enveloped the house, so intense, it felt unnatural. A framed picture of a younger Cress-man with a woman standing beside him sat on a table nearby. The silver frame glittered in the light of the room; it looked cold and, if not for the picture in it, impersonal.

"My wife," Cressman said; he had come up behind Brannigan.

"Very pretty. Do you have children?"

"No." Cressman gave him a long look. "We did. A son. He died when he was small."

"That must have been very difficult." Brannigan's words were automatic, perfunctory. He listened for nuances, for what the man wasn't saying.

"It was." Cressman looked steadily into Brannigan's eyes.

"It must have been devastating for your wife too. Is she here?"

"No. She died some time back." Cressman's expression remained confrontational. He and Brannigan stood very nearly eye to eye, but tension bristled between them as if they were two circling dogs.

"That's too bad. It must get lonely out here."

"It can. I've made adjustments."

Brannigan asked, "What adjustments?" It was brash, he knew, even rude, but he felt the situation would go nowhere if he didn't act. And, at the back of his mind, he wondered if those "adjustments" included finding another woman.

Cressman's reaction shone in his eyes; tension filled the room. An anniversary clock on the mantel ticked loudly, the only sound in the room.

"Are you finished?" Cressman asked.

Brannigan looked down at the glass of water in his hand, raised it, and drained it.

"You get into Pecos very often?" Brannigan asked as he handed the glass over to Cressman.

"Pecos?" The change in conversation clearly threw him. "Sometimes. Why?"

Brannigan eyed him. "Have you ever seen this telegram before?" He pulled it from his pocket.

Cressman looked at it briefly. "No. Why would I?"

"I was told you sent it." Brannigan stared at Cressman. His eyes never left the man's face. He knew as sure as he was standing there that the man was lying. The question was, why?

"Who told you that?"

"The woman in the Western Union office." Brannigan continued to watch Cressman's face carefully. "She said you sent this telegram for the woman in the picture."

Cressman studied Brannigan's face. He didn't smile. "It slipped my mind." He hesitated and then tried to affect a casual demeanor. "There was a young lady in Pecos who asked me to send a telegram for her."

"A perfect stranger? Why would she do that?"

"I don't know. I didn't ask her. I guess it was because she had her hands full. With her kids."

"She had kids with her?"

"She did. She had two of them. One was a baby, you know, not walking yet."

"Why didn't she send it herself?" Brannigan asked, suspicious.

"I told you. She had her hands full. She was struggling with the kids. They were small children, and they were fussing. I guess she didn't want to take them into the store."

"That seems strange, doesn't it?"

"No. Not particularly. She needed help. I helped her. People are neighborly around here. I remember I was glad that she didn't need help changing a tire." Cressman manufactured a laugh. It didn't ring true, and Brannigan didn't respond in kind.

"Did you see where she went after that?"

"No. She got back into her car and drove away. I didn't notice which direction she went." Cressman walked to the door and opened it. "Sorry I can't help you further."

Brannigan looked at him carefully. "So am I," he said.

When Brannigan turned around and headed away from the house, he looked back and saw Cressman watching him openly from a window. He jerked the gearshift into drive and sped away, kicking up a trail of dust behind him. He gave the rancher something to watch, knowing even as he sped away that his reaction was juvenile and not worthy of him. On the road, he headed back toward town and wondered what his next stop should be. Was it possible that he'd come all this far to gain nothing? When he reached the dusty little town, he continued on, driving straight through.

Chapter Twenty-three

Disposable diapers made dismal fans, Susan discovered as she sat in a corner of the cabin's porch and fanned herself with an unused diaper, the one thing she had readily at hand. The heat had grown unbearable even in the shade, and the cabin, as well as the scenery, had lost any rustic charm it might have had earlier. Chrissy and Bryan lay asleep on a quilt. No air circulated inside the cabin and very little outside. The whine of cicadas in the mesquite trees by the ravine remained the only sound for miles around. The whining noise the insects made rubbing their legs together to cool off in the heat—a sort of built-in ventilation system—was ambient all through the South.

The noise had no effect on the sleeping children. Bryan had explored outside around the cabin until Susan forced him to stay on the porch to avoid the sun. Keeping the two of them entertained took every ounce of her creative energy in the heat. Chrissy fell asleep first, but Bryan fought the very idea of rest. Perpetual motion was his favorite thing. The trick was to get him still long enough for him to fall asleep. She'd accomplished that by convincing him to watch the colony of red ants beside the porch. His fascination with nature drew him to stretch out on the porch to watch as the ants scurried about, endlessly toiling at their work. After a while Susan had pushed his hair back from his damp face and found him asleep. The face, a mirror image of his father's, created an unexpected pang

126

of longing in her. She'd moved Bryan to the quilt and then leaned back against the front outside wall of the cabin and allowed herself to be immersed in memories.

A clear picture of Kevin formed in her mind—the memory of a morning when she woke up early and saw him sleeping beside her. She'd discovered something so completely natural in his face as he slept. Stripped of his defenses and of any need to overplay his strength, which seemed to be common in his chosen profession, he'd exuded a human quality that touched her. Men spent so much energy being men, often unwilling to let anyone, especially other men, see sensitivity or tenderness in them. Kevin became more real in those moments when he let his guard down. She remembered touching his face and running her fingers down his chin onto his bare shoulder and arm. Sometimes, at the oddest moments, just looking at him would make her heart race. She'd run her fingertips lightly over the muscles of his upper arm. Her fingertips moved down his chest almost of their own volition and onto his taut stomach muscles. She hadn't known when he first woke up, but he grabbed her wrist, and suddenly the two of them were rolling across the bed and laughing together. Kevin pinned her down with his body weight and smiled. He had kissed her then, and she could remember now, these many months later, sitting on this porch in the heat of the West Texas afternoon, the exact feel of the warmth between them.

Chrissy woke, wet and hungry, and dragged Susan from her reverie. She got the diaper bag and pulled out the baby wipes and another diaper. Chrissy looked up at her with a fretful face. She cared more about eating than she did about being dry, but Susan changed the wet diaper first anyway. She looked out on the land as she fed Chrissy. Nothing stirred for miles around. Two tears dotted the baby's cheeks but began to dry as she felt warm milk fill her small stomach.

Once Chrissy was satisfied and again lying on the quilt, Susan sat dreamily half dozing with Chrissy beside her playing with the strap of the diaper bag. The red and blue whimsical figures on the bag entertained her and kept her baby fingers busy as she tried in vain to pluck them off.

Susan reached into the bag for a butterfly clip and twisted her hair up on top of her head and clipped it, something she should have done earlier, and she pulled a bottle of water from the picnic supplies. Time passed, but Susan had no idea how to clock it. She'd forgotten her watch, and her cell phone with its constantly accurate time had long since been taken from her. Time had lost its meaning anyway since she'd been at the ranch. How long had she been at the ranch? How many days? She didn't even know; the days had blurred one into another. How many days had it been since she'd left the safety of their home on the base? And why had Cressman sent her out here? One thing for sure, it was not to see another part of the ranch. Why had he deserted her here?

Bryan woke up hungry, and Susan found an apple among the picnic food and cut it up for him. What had prompted the urge for this picnic, she wondered. A picnic was something people did for fun. Where was the fun in this picnic? And why had John thought they would like this? This was more like an extension of their prison, only with fresh air. Very hot, fresh air. And she didn't want to think of Cressman as John. Using his first name personalized him and made him more intimate somehow.

She'd heard of kidnap victims identifying with their kidnappers, even drawing close to them. Human beings were adaptable. *Oh, dear God*, she pleaded, closing her eyes, *don't let me do that. Please. Don't let me add disgrace to the stupidity that got me into this situation to begin with. I have to think of a way to get us out of here,* she thought for what felt like the hundredth time. She shut her eyes as tightly as she could and squeezed the unwanted tears from between her lashes. When she opened them, she saw a dust cloud and wondered for just a moment if she had conjured it up out of need, because the dust cloud on the horizon was moving in her direction.

The cloud grew larger until it materialized into a pickup

truck—the newer of the two trucks she'd seen around the ranch. It pulled up close to the porch of the old cabin, and John Cressman stepped out of the air-conditioned cab, cool and fresh and smiling. Susan looked at him from her seat on the old porch where she sat with perspiration trickling down her neck. She had nothing to say to him.

Mendoza beat the bushes, figuratively, trying to find clues to the whereabouts of Brannigan's wife, but he had the disadvantage of geography. Where could she be? Before Brannigan discovered that she'd contacted her sister and had been en route to Phoenix, he'd checked everywhere in the immediate area. No one knew a thing, not one scrap of information, useful or otherwise. Women didn't just disappear off the map, did they?

He'd seen the two of them together in the past; the Brannigans had appeared to be happy. What had gone wrong? Brannigan had screwed up somehow, poor schmuck. He could make it better, surely. But to make it better, he had to find her.

Mendoza felt grateful for the relative peace in his own home. Lydia was always glad to see him when he got home. Whether it was at the end of the day or the end of a mission, she greeted him with the same warmth. But Lyddie had a warm heart. Brannigan's wife distanced herself from the crowd. Or was it that she was a little shy? Now she was gone. *Poof.* Just like that. He didn't know what he'd do if it was Lyddie out there somewhere, missing. Probably the same things Brannigan was doing. He'd engage in the same frantic behavior too.

Those thoughts culminated as he pulled up to Brannigan's quarters to check his mail. Stuffed full—the lid on the box couldn't even close. *Please, God, let there be something from Brannigan's wife. One little envelope, that's all I ask for,* he thought. *A note, just a little note.*

Mendoza thumbed through the mail, oddly uncomfortable checking through correspondence that wasn't his. He stole a glance toward the street to see if anyone noticed what he was doing. Junk mail, offers—*you're pre-approved for yet another credit card*—advertisements, two letters, neither from Brannigan's wife, a book from a Dr. Seuss book club, and a credit card bill. Mendoza stared at the envelope. It was a bill from a *gasoline* credit card. *What if?* Mendoza slammed the box shut and hurried to his car with the mail. As he did, he reached for his cell phone.

Chapter Twenty-four

Brannigan drove all the way to the Mountain View Motel in Pecos without so much as braking the car. He unlocked the door, turned the air conditioner down, then sat on the bed, his back against the headboard. What should he do now? What could he do? Should he admit defeat? Should he pack up and go home? Where was home if Susan wasn't there? And the kids. Should he accept the obvious fact that Susan had left him? He flinched at the thought but forced his mind to consider it. The one thing that would make sense of it would be the very thing he least wanted to believe. If Susan had left him and did not want to be found, that would explain why she'd left no note, no message anywhere, and why he could find no trace of her.

He reached for the phone and called Mendoza. The unanswered ringing irritated him till he slammed the receiver back onto the cradle. He jumped up and began to pace across the floor. *What is going on? What is it I'm missing? What is it that's staring me in the face? Why can't I fit this together?*

Brannigan called Susan's sister again, but Sharon had heard nothing from Susan, and, to add to his misery, she told him that her parents were so worried, they were ill. Brannigan cut the call short. He couldn't discuss how painful this was for anyone else. All that did was double his guilt. Susan was his wife. His. He leaned against the headboard and thought about it. He knew what her parents thought, or he could guess. They thought Susan had left him because he'd been insensitive and

inconsiderate. Maybe he had been insensitive. But he still
could not believe she'd left him. That made it so cut-and-
dried, so definite. How could they work it out with her gone?
How could they make it better?

The phone rang beside him, and he jumped for it, glad to
hear Mendoza's voice. "I tried to call you earlier," Brannigan
said without feeling.

"Sorry, I had to drop Lyddie over at the base day care—her
car is in the shop—and then I went by to check your place,
and I picked up your mail. Anything new?"

"No. I checked it out, all of it, and I came up with zilch.
Nada. I've gone as far as I can go here. Some of it doesn't add
up, but I guess I'll have to face the obvious fact. She left me,
and it looks like she doesn't want to be found."

"I'm still bettin' you'll hear from her," Mendoza said.

"Or her lawyer," Brannigan added.

"It isn't going to come to that. She'll contact you, and once
she does, the two of you will have a chance to work it out. She'll
have to get in touch; she'll need more things from the house,
won't she? And money?"

"Eventually. Is there any sign that she'd been back at the
house?"

"No. Everything's the same. I got the mail and went in to
check around. It looks the same as it did when you left it."

"And the mail?"

"There's nothing from your wife," Mendoza said reluc-
tantly. "But there is something from your Exxon credit card."

"Exxon? The statement from Exxon?"

"Yes. Do you think—?"

A sudden excitement charged through the line. "Open it,"
Brannigan told him, although he usually kept his business to
himself. He could hear the envelope ripping all those miles
away. "Well?" he prompted.

"It's a good thing you make more money than I do," Mendoza quipped, but Brannigan was in no mood for parleying
quips.

"Never mind that," he said. "Look at the list of charges and where they're from."

"I'm looking. The list is long. The first ones are from around here, of course. Here—here's one from Al's Exxon in Atlanta. Here's one in Shreveport." Mendoza's voice rose in expectation with each discovery. "Another in Dallas. Here! There's one from Pecos, Texas. It looks like it's the most recent charge, but it's dated more than two weeks ago."

"What's the name of the place?"

"Johnson's Exxon on I-20. I don't see anything on the list after that date."

Pecos again, Brannigan thought. Everything led to Pecos. But after Pecos, nothing. What had happened in Pecos? "I'm going over to that gas station to see if I can find out anything there. I'll also call Exxon to see if there were any charges that came in after the billing date. If I don't learn anything, then"— he hesitated; he hated to say it, but he did—"I'll come home."

Johnson's Exxon was easy to find out on Interstate 20. Brannigan pulled into the driveway and climbed out into the hot and dusty afternoon. He found his expectations rising again but tried to suppress them in case they led to more disappointment. But he soon discovered it was impossible to squelch his expectations altogether, or his hope.

A tall, thin boy sat in the office when Brannigan walked in. He had propped his long legs up on a battered desk and played with a hand-held electronic game, so absorbed he didn't notice anyone was there. Brannigan waited but said nothing. Finally the boy looked up and asked, "Need a fill-up?"

"No, just some information." Brannigan pulled the snapshot from his pocket. Would he ever be able to end this new, unfortunate habit of identifying Susan through this photo? "I'm looking for someone," he said for what felt like the hundredth time. "She stopped in here just over two weeks ago."

The kid looked at the picture carefully. "I don't know, Mister. I might have seen her. She looks a little familiar, but we get a lot

of people in here, you know? I mean, since we're on the Interstate, and there ain't another place to get gas for a lotta miles."

"She would have had two kids with her. A baby and a boy
who's three."

"I just don't remember. I'm sorry." He looked sorry too, his
thin face sympathetic.

An old red pickup passed by emitting a series of honks,
whoops, and a cloud of black smoke. The boy waved at the
tangle of arms protruding from the truck's windows. He grinned
and explained unnecessarily, "Friends of mine." Then he gave
the picture back to Brannigan and told him, "Wish I could help
you."

"Who else works here? Maybe I could talk to them?"

"Naw, there's just me and my dad. He's over in Van Horn
today, and he won't be back till late."

"All right." Brannigan turned to go and said, "Thanks."
Useless, he thought. *No sense in pursuing it any further.* There
was nothing to go on anyway.

He stood by the rental car and stared off down the highway
at a mirage of water across the road, the effect of heat shim-
mering in the distance. Were his chances of finding Susan like
that water in the distance—the closer he got, the more elusive
it became? Was she even now gone from his life forever? Had
their life together disappeared already, destined to become
only a memory? And was he just too stubborn or too stupid to
realize it?

Brannigan got into the car and turned the key, but before he
gave it gas, before the engine revved, the kid appeared beside
him, and Brannigan lowered the window. "Does the boy have
dark hair like yours?" the kid asked.

Brannigan's pulse surged. "Yes." He turned the motor off.

"And the baby was real little—I mean, not walking or anything. In one of those car seats for babies?"

"Yes. You saw them?"

"Well, there was this lady a while back. I don't remember
what day. She was a real babe; she had long blond hair and a

really hot body, but she had kids, so I figured she must be married. Anyway, the little boy was a cute kid. He kept hanging out the window talking to me. I probably wouldn't have remembered them except for the problem with the car."

"What problem with the car?"

"When she drove off, I saw this puddle where her car had been. I tried to stop her, but I guess she didn't see me in the rearview mirror. That puddle was water or, you know, that coolant stuff. That's what bothered me most. She was headed west on a hot day, and her car was losing water."

"You didn't see her again?"

"No. I thought I might, because I didn't think she could get far with that much water leakin'. But she never came back."

"Do you remember the car?" This was the big question, the final proof.

"Yeah." The boy squinted and stared off into the distance as if that would jog his memory. "It was one of those small SUVs—you know the kind. And it was white, I think."

Bingo, Brannigan thought. Yeah, he knew the kind. He had bought it for Susan. *This was it!* Aloud he said, "Thanks. You've been a big help."

"No problem." The kid ambled back to the office and picked up his game.

Car trouble. Why hadn't Brannigan considered that possibility? Mendoza had even mentioned it once, he remembered now. If the cooling system had been leaking, it would be only a matter of time before the engine overheated. Once it overheated, it would stall. Where would that leave her? Brannigan stared down at the map as perspiration trickled down his neck. The little dot representing Fleming leaped out at him. He sat staring at it, the almost forgotten little town bypassed by the highway and unimportant to everyone in the outside world. Almost everyone.

Now he followed his gut instinct. It was all that was left to him. He leaned forward, turned the key in the ignition, and drove west.

Chapter Twenty-five

Susan lay in the hazy netherworld between sleep and reality when the door cracked and a sliver of light broke into the room. It widened until it reached the bed, and she tensed, seeing yet not seeing the light behind closed eyelids. When had it begun, this stealthy voyeurism, this clandestine watching of her while she lay sleeping? She had no idea; she had become aware of it only in the last two nights.

John Cressman stood in the doorway and stared at her, uttering no sound. His breathing filled the room. Susan tried through narrow slits of partially opened eyes to read his expression, but she was unable to. On some inexplicable level, she knew that it would be dangerous for her to acknowledge his presence.

Cressman moved across the room and stood beside the bed.

Would he reach out for her, and, if he did, what then? What would be his reaction if she opened her eyes and demanded to know what he was doing there? Her heart hammered, slamming her rib cage as she realized he had become increasingly erratic. Was he facing down a delusional episode? Would he snap and hurt her? Would he hurt the children?

As he had the night before, he touched the sheet lying across her body, and she sensed the struggle within him. He turned abruptly and left the room, closing the door behind him. For a long while Susan lay in the bed with her eyes open, stared at the darkness, and tried to quiet her breathing.

* * *

The short row of businesses had few lights and appeared more desolate than before, now that they were closed and devoid of life. The glow from two or three neon signs penetrated the darkness no more than a few feet in the midnight hour. Brannigan parked the rental car in the shadow of an abandoned building, an antiquated gas station. He sat still for what seemed an interminable length of time and waited to see if anyone had observed his arrival. There was no sign of movement, and there had been none since he drove into town. He sat in quiet thought, searching for . . . what? What his next step should be? His attention became focused on the gas station, not the old one next to him with its rusting pumps and rotting boards, but the one where he'd stopped when he first came into town. The odd looks he'd received from the station owner and his wife, the waitress at the café, were unexplained and still disturbed him. There had been something slightly off-key with these people, although they'd appeared friendly enough until they knew why he was there.

He studied the gas station, the only working one in town. If her car had broken down, Susan would have had no choice but to deal with the only garage in town. As near as he could tell, the garage and gas station were one and the same. Brannigan eased open the car door with as little noise as possible and crossed the road to the operational gas station. The front door would not give when he pushed it. Locked. Of course. He rounded the back of the building, discovered a door, and tried it. Locked up tightly also. He'd always heard that no one worried about locking doors in small towns. Perhaps these small-town residents weren't all that friendly after all.

A few feet past the door was a solitary window. Brannigan tried it and felt it lift easily enough. Not much use locking the doors, Ed, old man. One push, and Brannigan was in. Flashing his penlight for a brief second, he discovered he was in a bathroom. A bathroom sorely in need of paint but surprisingly clean. The bathroom door squeaked when he opened it, and the sound pierced the night. He paused as the blood pumped rapidly in his head, and his muscles tensed. He waited for someone, anyone, some night owl who had heard the noise and would come rushing to investigate. No one appeared. The night played on as peacefully as before, and his heart began to slow to somewhere within normal range.

Once inside, Brannigan crept down a short hall and faced the garage. Tools hung along the walls, and a tarp-covered vehicle sat in a bay, parts strewn along the hood. He moved toward the office carefully, stepping over tires and a jack. The office was only a small portion of the building and devoid of any personal items. A brief flash of light illuminated a desk and a file cabinet, a couple of chairs. The drawers of the file cabinet were not locked, but they were a jumble of miscellaneous items, outdated paperwork, coffee cups, and even small car parts.

On the desk a spindle held a stack of work orders dating weeks back. Brannigan pulled a few off the top; the information appeared sketchy, some filled in, others not. It would appear that Ed was not very organized. Brannigan pulled the remainder of the papers off the spindle and looked at them, but he stopped halfway through and stared at the slip he held in his hand. He would have missed it altogether if it hadn't been for the license-plate number. There was no name written at the top, but the work order called for a radiator to be replaced. It was marked PAID IN FULL, and the date was sixteen days earlier. Brannigan recognized the plate number; he'd put those very plates on the car just two months earlier.

Susan had been here. The SUV had broken down, and she'd come to this godforsaken place to get it repaired. What then? Where had she gone from here? And how did the rancher fit into it? If the overheating had occurred near Fleming, how did that explain Susan's meeting up with the rancher outside the Western Union in Pecos?

A shadow moved in the night, and Brannigan doused the light and put the work orders back onto the spindle by feel. He stood in the dark and watched the shadow cross the road. The figure stumbled once, picked himself up, and ambled toward the side door of the building across the street.

Brannigan headed back through the garage and pushed through the open window to leave, but then he stopped. Something nagged at him. A memory? No, not a memory, not even that, more like a flash of sensory perception. He slid back into the bathroom, his foot narrowly missing the toilet.

In the garage he found that he reacted exactly as he did on recon. His mouth turned dry, and the hair along the back of his neck stood on end in anticipation of something unforeseen. He was like the proverbial teen creeping down the basement stairs in a slasher movie. Brannigan flashed the light in the direction of the tarp he'd seen earlier. Sitting on the tarpaulin was the object he'd spotted earlier but hadn't focused on long enough to realize what it meant. A radiator with a good-sized hole in it drew him across the garage. Brannigan bent over and pulled the edge of the tarp back to expose the car underneath. An SUV, small and white. He didn't need to go to the back of the SUV and expose the plates to know. He didn't need to, but he did it anyway. South Carolina plates. He pulled the tarp off and looked into the car. The car was empty, not a personal item in sight. Cleaned out completely. Seeing the car brought back the pain he had felt when he'd first found Susan and the kids missing. He wanted to shout, *Where are you, Susan? Where are you?*

Brannigan pulled the tarp back into place till it covered the car completely, and then he got out of there. He had a legal right to the car, but this wasn't about the car. It hadn't been the car he had come so many miles to find. He crept back out of the building, listening for anyone who might be about. When he reached his rental car, he started the engine and drove out of the town for the second time. He left knowing full well that Susan and the children had to be nearby. He wanted to wake up the townspeople, wake them and demand that his family be given back to him. Instead, he drove straight back to the motel in Pecos and called Mendoza's number. He needed help. He knew that now, and he knew he needed it quickly.

Mendoza answered the phone right after the first ring. "Yeah?"

Brannigan looked at his watch—2:00 A.M., which meant it was 3:00 A.M. in Lejeune. "I guess I woke you."

"That would be a good guess."

"I had to call." The level of excitement Brannigan felt would keep him from sleep, he knew. He had to share it with someone, and who better than Mendoza?

"You found her." It was a statement, not a question. On his end, with little more to go on, Mendoza felt the muscles in his face pull into a grin, the first in a long while.

"No, but I found something else. I found the car."

"You found the car? Her car? Where?"

"Remember the town I told you about? Fleming? The one near the ranch?"

"Yes." An involuntary yawn hit Mendoza, complete with sound, and he mumbled, "Sorry, honey, I'll take it in the other room." Muffled noises, the sound of a door closing, and the rattle of glass on metal refrigerator shelves. Mendoza had gone into the kitchen. Brannigan's life was on the dung heap, but he'd found his first real and solid clue; he was excited. And Mendoza was getting a snack. "Okay, sorry," Mendoza said. "You found the car."

"It's there. It's in the garage covered with a tarp. The radiator is out; a new one has been ordered. I found the work order too."

"Wait, how'd you know where to look? Who told you?"

"Remember the bill? I went to the gas station and talked to the kid who'd pumped her gas."

"He remembered her?"

"Wouldn't you?" Brannigan asked.

"Good point," Mendoza conceded. "But how did he know where to find her?"

"He didn't, but what he did remember was that the car was leaking coolant when she drove off. I figured it must have overheated not too long after that, and she would choose the closest town for help."

"And that led you to Fleming?"

"Yes, *and* there's only one garage in Fleming. You have to see this town; it's a spot in the road."

"So you went to the garage again?"

"Well"—Brannigan hesitated—"I scoped it out. They wouldn't tell me anything the first time, so I went back after everything closed down."

"You 'went back'? Meaning, you broke in?"

Brannigan hedged. "More or less."

"You broke in?" Mendoza couldn't believe what he was hearing.

"I had to know."

Mendoza was fully awake now, and he was afraid to hear Brannigan's next statement. He didn't have to ask.

Brannigan told him, "Now I have to get onto that ranch."

"What?" The one word was, like Mendoza's reaction, explosive.

"I have to get onto that ranch. She's there, or the cowboy knows where she is. I feel it in my gut."

"You can't go there. He'll toss you out. And if it's a working ranch, he's got men working for him; he must have. You'd better go to the police."

"And say what? That a man I never heard of has my wife at his ranch and won't let me see her? And that I know she's there because I found her car when I broke into the garage in the town nearby?"

"Okay, I get your point, but what makes you think the rancher will let you in?"

"I wasn't going to ask. What I need is a new face in a new car, because the only way to reach the ranch is to drive right through the middle of town. And this isn't a place that gets many visitors. The whole town will notice if I go back there."

"A new face?" Mendoza asked, already sensing the implication.

"Someone who's never been seen in this area. Someone who can go across terrain. Someone who could carry high-powered binoculars, maybe even a camera with a zoom lens to get proof that she's there. Someone I can trust to do all that and bring me the proof."

There was silence on the line for a long while as Mendoza debated his next words and the advisability of playing devil's advocate with a man as desperate as Brannigan. But they'd always been straight with each other. "Have you considered the possibility that she may have asked the rancher not to tell you where she is?"

Brannigan found it difficult to say, but he admitted it. "Yes. I've thought of that."

"And?"

"She owes me an explanation, and there's the other thing."

"What other thing?"

"My children."

Another silence. Mendoza thought about illegal procedures, about the possibility of being caught. What Brannigan asked of him was not that much different than what they did for a living. And Mendoza was very good at it. He let out a breath. "I'll check for a flight, and I'll call you back."

"Do you need money? You may have to take a commercial flight if you can't get a hop. I need you to get here ASAP."

"No. I've got it. If my expenses get too high, I'll let you know."

They left it at that.

Sunlight streamed across the table and gave a deceptively warm glow to the strained atmosphere. Susan looked at the breakfast tacos on her plate. They looked good, but her nerves were strained to the breaking point and had left her without any sign of an appetite. John sat at the table watching her. Bryan ate his breakfast eagerly and stopped only to talk about the puppies and the calf in the barn. He took bites out of the middle of his taco, creating a hole that caused the potatoes and eggs to fall through. She wondered if he missed his favorite breakfast food—Cheerios. She hadn't seen a Cheerio in weeks. Chrissy sat in the high chair that John had brought from storage and fingered the cut-up pieces of banana on her tray.

"She's doing very well with regular food," John said. He referred to the meals of soft food Chrissy had eaten recently. Susan looked at him. He sounded like any normal, interested father. That was what frightened her.

"I wish you would eat something. The children are doing fine."

"The children are too young to understand what's going on."

"They're happy here." He smiled at her. "They have you, and they have all this." He swept his arm toward the open room.

Susan gave up. She had tried several times to reach him rationally, but he never seemed to hear her. She looked at him now. He had to be in his late fifties—his hair was completely white—but the ranch work kept his body toned. Only his stomach had softened and filled out a little. Maybe that was obvious only because it perched above straight hips and long, thin legs. For his ranch work Cressman wore jeans and a work shirt and left his fancy belt buckles off. Instead, he wore a leather belt with a hand-tooled design of Texas longhorns on either side and his monogram across the back. Handling cattle, riding horseback, pitching hay, filling troughs daily to circumvent the scarcity of water was all hard physical work. Cressman had ten to twelve men working the ranch, but he could have used twenty. He put his sweat into the place daily, and his back obviously ached along with the rest of the men's when they finished at night. It was a hard life, maybe the only one he'd ever known, but Susan wondered why he kept doing it year after year. What drove him? As far as Susan could see, he derived little pleasure from his chosen life.

Cressman noticed Susan studying him and tried again for

conversation. "She really likes that banana." This, as Chrissy smeared banana on her chin. "She's ready for regular food completely. She's doing so well, she could take the bottle. Or even a cup."

Susan searched his face for meaning. "She's mastered bananas and cereal and mashed carrots. It's a slow process."

"I remember," he said.

Susan had forgotten about the son he'd lost, but she didn't want to talk about it with him, or about anything else for that matter. She stood up and took Chrissy out of the high chair. "I'm going to clean her up. I'm not very hungry anyway." To Bryan she said, "Come on, Bryan. Let's wash your hands."

As she passed Cressman's chair, he stood up abruptly and grabbed her arm. He came close, his body size and intent threatening. Bryan stopped and looked from his mother to his new friend and then back to his mother's face. Something was wrong.

"We'll talk about this again. I'm a patient man, Susan, but even I have my limits. You'd better make some effort here and start adapting. Get outside, take a walk, go swim in the pool, do something while the kids are napping. You understand?"

His eyes narrowed, hardened, and the reaction was a surge of adrenaline in her body. The fear grew so strong, she could taste it.

He seemed to sense her reaction, but he gripped her and pushed her against the wall roughly. "Don't make me hurt you, Susan. I don't want to hurt you."

She didn't answer, and when she tried to walk away, he stopped her and said, as if it was just a suggestion, "Yes. That's a good idea. You get outside for a while. Maria will take care of the children. Fresh air and swimming will improve your appetite. Then you and I can have a late dinner tonight, just the two of us." Cressman noticed that Bryan was watching them, and he released her wrist.

Susan left him, her fingers trembling, and went into the bedroom. She sat on the bed and held her babies. Bryan looked at her, unable to understand, his little face worried. Chrissy, oblivious to the tension, reached banana-smeared fingers into Susan's hair. Susan's one abiding thought was how to end this nightmare.

Chapter Twenty-six

Cressman assumed that all it would take for Susan to adjust was more time. Was the man delusional? He *had* to be if he thought she could so easily forget her husband and the life they'd shared. She and Kevin hadn't been married long, but their relationship had developed and deepened, and the two children had added to that bond. But then, somewhere along the way, they'd hit some bumps in the road of their relationship. Had they let their lives become mundane, even bleak? When had that happened and why? Was it the everyday grind of life that eroded their marriage, the everyday let's-just-get-through-the-day-and-all-its-related-activities? Or had they simply neglected to take time for each other? Had they let the time away from each other, imposed by his military career and the constant round of diaper-changing, feeding, laundry, and so much more, get in the way of their actually seeing and reveling in each other? Had their lives revolved solely around the needs of the children, ignoring their own? The children had introduced an immediacy to life—all children did. Their needs had to be taken care of and often had to come first. Had she and Kevin grown accustomed to neglecting themselves while tending the children? But, regardless of the nature or current status of their relationship, Cressman had no right to interfere with any of it, or them.

His attitude was invasive and overbearing, not to mention the fact that everything else was criminal. Had the man experienced a psychotic breakdown? Some break with reality altogether? When he looked at her with his penetrating eyes, she wanted to run in the opposite direction, but when he stated calmly that she needed to stop breastfeeding *his* child—the *his* meaning Kevin's—she wanted to fight.

After their late dinner that night without the children, Cressman towered over her, and his proprietary attitude scared her more than a little. Susan felt as if she had stepped into a new form of the *Twilight Zone* where she alone looked at things as they really were. More than once Cressman had grabbed her, and the heat from his body, the physical need, threatened her. Each time she tried to remove herself, to create more space between them, to break the spell he seemed to be under, but he would grab her forearm and pull her so close, she could see the pupils of his eyes contract.

Now he appeared calm, and he said, "Maria is here to clear the dishes away. We'll continue our discussion later."

Discussion? What discussion? They had dined in near silence.

And then, in spite of what he'd said, he didn't let her go. Beads of perspiration broke out above his upper lip, and he stared at her with an intensity that frightened her thoroughly, all the way down to her toes. Three times she tried to pull away, to pry her arms loose from his grip, but to no avail. He was not a young man, but his strength was more than she'd expected.

Cressman finally loosened his hold with his right hand but he kept a tight rein with the left and then moved his right hand to splay against her rib cage, and at that point Susan's fear turned to anger and then to pure, unadulterated rage. She wanted to hit him, to gouge his eyes out. She'd never felt such rage in her life. When Cressman saw it in her eyes, he smiled, seemingly glad to have evoked some sort of passion in her at last. At his smile she only grew angrier, but he had her pinned close to him.

Susan strained her neck to look at Maria bent over the table, stacking plates. Maria's eyes were downcast; did she think she'd walked in on a tête-à-tête? Couldn't she feel the tension in the room? Susan would get no help from Maria or from anyone else on the ranch. There was no hope in that direction. The workers had paychecks to think about, and it would not take a wild guess to realize jobs were scarce in this part of the world.

Susan had an idea, and she stepped closer to Cressman and placed both feet on the toe of his boot. With all of her weight on his foot, a slight grimace crossed his face. He started to ease her off, but as he did, she brought her knee up to his groin. But Cressman's reflexes were too fast; he grabbed her knee and deflected it toward his thigh, and he looked as if he enjoyed it. *What a jerk!* She was dumbfounded, and just as she strained to hurt him again, in any way she could, he dropped her knee and pushed her back so abruptly, she nearly fell.

"Enough," he said. "For now." He backed up several feet and said, "We'll spar later."

Spar? What was wrong with the man? Was that what this was? *Sparring?* Only in his mind, she thought.

"Go check on the children." He had dismissed her.

Susan wanted to retaliate verbally if not physically, but she felt diminished and dirty somehow. She crept back into the room where her babies were playing, and she rocked herself in the big old rocking chair. The rage had deserted her and left her spent, emotionally as well as physically. The lunacy of Cressman's behavior had escalated; she had to do something before it grew worse. But what?

Susan was on that ranch. She had to be. Kevin could think of nothing else. He wanted to smash something or grab hold of someone and choke the life out of him. He hadn't felt like this in a long time, and he recognized it for what it was, suppressed frustration and rage. She'd been taken from him, as surely as if predators had come into their home during the night and torn her from his grasp. In his rage all remembrance of her leaving was erased, and he only knew that he wanted her back.

Chapter Twenty-seven

How could anyone deal with this isolation? Susan had always lived in places where she could walk down the street and find some form of public transportation if she wanted it. Life in the city offered all sorts of amenities, and she loved all the potential for things to do, places to go, and a means to get there. The country had an appeal; she valued it even more now that she had children—the quiet, the space, the fresh air, and more—but this was too much. Miles of open land with nothing but low shrubs and very few trees, this land had a stark beauty of its own but was too isolated for her taste.

Had it been the isolation that had worked on Cressman till it robbed him of his reasoning or his grip on reality? He had no family, no close relatives to share the ranch with, and in that case losing his wife and son might have been an even greater tragedy than Susan had first imagined. Had the loneliness and isolation been more than he could bear? Had Cressman's contact with reality been tenuous already? Or had it been the loneliness that did the most damage? And then she realized what she was doing; *she was thinking about him, identifying with him.* She didn't care what had caused him to go off-kilter. All she cared about was getting away from him!

As she pondered the isolation and loneliness, Cressman came to the door again and watched the children playing on the floor. Was he remorseful over the way he'd manhandled her? He didn't look it. Had he already dismissed the way he'd

149

treated her? She couldn't tell. She stared at him, and as she stared at him and gathered her resolve, her chin rose. She would not be a victim. *I will not be a victim.* That would be her new mantra.

Susan picked the baby up off the floor and held her so close that Chrissy squirmed. Bryan poured Lego blocks onto Susan's lap and across Chrissy's feet, and the baby giggled. He picked up additional blocks and christened the baby's feet with them again, and she giggled some more.

Cressman looked in on the scene with an intense longing in his eyes, but he turned and left without a word. What was he thinking now? Was he formulating new plans even as Susan sat and accomplished nothing in her effort to escape the ranch? Each new day filled her with dread, and she had to wonder, what might that day bring?

Brannigan lay on the bed in the motel room and waited for the hours to tick away. How much of his life had been spent in waiting? In the military, troops were often required to wait—for the next meal, for the right time for maneuvers, for transport. He remembered waiting to learn if his first child was a boy or girl. He'd secretly wanted a boy but was reluctant to say it out loud. Would it have offended Susan? She said she didn't mind if he preferred a boy, but he knew she didn't understand how strong his desire for a son was. He'd been so happy to hear that the baby was a boy, and then he'd waited while Susan was in labor. The wait had been long, but they'd been connected, one in purpose if not in effort. That was something he would remember always, one of the defining moments of his life, of their lives. Lesson learned. He would be more sensitive. He hadn't known what love really was until he met Susan. From the first he had wanted to be with her all the time, and he was happiest during the moments that he spent with her, whether they were eating out at a fancy restaurant or planting bulbs for Susan's elderly neighbor. They never ran out of things to talk about or to do together, and somewhere along the way he'd known he wanted to be with her the rest of their lives, to have children with her, and to grow old together.

And now she was gone, and he sat waiting and hoping that he could find her, because if he could, maybe, just maybe, he would discover that she hadn't left him. Maybe he would learn that they still had that connection, that he hadn't screwed up their life and shattered it altogether. But he wasn't one to sit and wait; he was used to action, and he jumped up and rushed toward the door. He wanted to take matters into his own hands, but when his hand clenched the doorknob, he forced himself to stop. He began to pace the floor. Was there something he could do while he waited for Mendoza? With his adrenaline surging, he felt he could tear that ranch apart with his bare hands. And the rancher too.

Chapter Twenty-eight

Susan took the suggestion that she get out and get fresh air while the children napped, but only because she'd reached the limit of her endurance; she could not stand being inside those walls another hour. The heat was so intense that it stifled her, and she sought refuge in the barn barely ten minutes out. The interior of the barn was cool by comparison because it offered shade. Susan had never gone to the barn alone because she had no interest in anything on the ranch except for a way to get off it. There was no one around, not even one of the ranch hands. The barn was quiet except for the occasional rustle of hoof movement in the hay or the whimpering of the puppies as they pushed at one another, greedy for their chance to eat. The beleaguered mama dog glanced at her offspring, her brows pulled together in puzzled apprehension, but she turned onto her side and stretched out, giving the puppies full access. She turned her head and looked up as Susan reached down and scratched the dog's ears. "Sorry, old girl. It isn't easy; I know."

The calf that Bryan loved dearly had grown since he had first shown it to her. Bryan had pulled her forward to see the calf as proudly as if it had been his own. The calf's large brown eyes looked up at her without reaction, and Susan marveled at the appeal of all baby animals. The calf's mother turned and glanced at Susan with a look of indifference before turning her attention back to her young.

Across the barn a mare stood alone in one of the larger stalls. "What are you in for?" she asked. The horse gave her a quizzical look, then turned away. She was a beautiful animal, her coat a deep strawberry bronze in color, her mane hanging long on her neck. Her body was sleek and healthy looking with muscular withers and shank. She sauntered to the gate and blinked at Susan, then leaned her head out over the top. Susan involuntarily shrank back. She'd always been a city girl, and even though she had loved horses as a youngster and read as many books as she could find about them, she'd had no real experience with them.

The mare stood still and eyed Susan with large and beautiful liquid brown eyes, and something in them made Susan relax and stretch a tentative hand out to touch the soft muzzle extended toward her. A patch of white hair grew along the bridge of the mare's face, running downward from a peak between her eyes. The large nostrils snorted softly, and Susan jumped. Her own movement caused a reaction in the horse, and she stepped back. Susan laughed at herself and the horse. "We're a pair, aren't we?" she said. "I don't know who's more nervous, you or me."

The mare stepped forward and leaned her head over the gate of her stall. Susan felt a kinship she'd never felt toward an animal before. She leaned her own head forward and laid her cheek against the mare's nose. The hair surprised her; it was not as soft as it appeared and yet not bristly, but it had a real strength to it. She breathed in the scent of horseflesh, that smell of sunshine and dust and freedom that most horses exude, and she wondered what it would be like to climb onto her back and take off, holding on to her long mane and riding out across the land forever. It would be freedom, a glorious freedom that need never end. Susan had never experienced that kind of freedom, but she liked to think this creature had. Perhaps that kind of freedom didn't exist anymore. Maybe it never had.

Susan pulled fresh straw up from a pile in a corner and put

it over the gate into the stall. The mare looked at Susan as if
she wondered what she was doing. Maybe it wasn't time for
hay. Susan had no idea when horses ate or how often. It occurred
to her to wonder if this horse could be her ticket to freedom. Not
out over the range but back toward the town to civilization, to
telephones and her car. Not all of the people in Fleming could be
in John Cressman's pocket. Not all of them knew what he'd
done and had kept quiet about it, surely.

But could she ride this horse? She looked around and saw a
saddle sitting on top of the rail of a stall. She looked at the
saddle closely and wondered if she could figure out how to put
it onto the horse. She'd seen westerns on TV. It couldn't be
that difficult, could it? If a saddle wasn't cinched properly on
the horse, it could result in a fall; she knew that much. Where
had she learned that? From a movie or a book? Did she dare
take that risk with Bryan and Chrissy along?

And the ride, her fabulous freedom ride, would have to be
at night. She hadn't a chance of getting away during the daylight with Cressman around. However much the thought of
saddling up a horse and riding it with her children terrified
her, staying at the ranch with a delusional cowboy who thought
she was a dead-ringer for his wife, not to mention a replacement for her, was even more terrifying.

Any escape would have to be planned and executed carefully. She had failed the first time, and after that experience
she'd thought John would install more locks or guards, but she
had seen no indication that anything had changed. And that
more than anything else made her realize how many obstacles
there were between her and escape. Factoring in the unpre-
dictability of an animal made Susan realize her chances were
risky, but she was never going to get out if she didn't take
risks. Kevin had no idea where she was. Was he even back
from his mission yet? If so, had he been looking for her? She
hoped he was, but there was nothing to lead him to this place,
even if he figured out where she'd been going. Susan thought

of Sharon. When Kevin couldn't find her, he would call her family. Sharon would tell him about their conversation, that Susan had been coming out to see her. But it was no use; there was no way he could find her. She would have to rely on herself to get free, and it had been long enough. She would wait until night, until the moonlight shone brightly enough for her to see, and then she would get herself and her children off this godforsaken place.

While Brannigan forced himself to wait for Mendoza, he had ample time to think, and his thoughts led him to several conclusions. One thing he knew for certain was that he wanted his wife back. If she had left him for good, he still held out hope that they could work it out. Susan loved him, and he held on to that thought, knowing that that could not change in so short a time. Another certainty was that he wanted his children—for him it was a package deal. He could never take them from their mother even if it came down to that, so the only plan was to get all three of them back. They were a family, and they only worked as a complete family. If he had to rethink some of his attitudes to make it happen, then that's what he'd do. He knew he wasn't entirely wrong in his dedication to his work, but he wasn't ready to sacrifice his personal life either. There had to be a balance, and he believed they could find it together.

He spent the early hours of the day pacing in the small room and rehashing everything Susan had said in their last argument. He considered calling Sharon again to ask what Susan had said to her, but it was difficult to hear about his personal life from a third person. He wondered how much Susan had said to her sister, but he was afraid to find out.

He switched his thoughts to his children, and he wondered if Bryan had asked for him. Did his son miss him, he wondered. Or, he forced himself to think, had he been gone so much that Bryan was equally happy when his father was out of the picture? That thought brought on a depression so intense that he had to get out of the motel, and it was all he could do to keep from driving back to the ranch and demanding to know where his wife and children were. He wanted to, but he didn't. Instead he drove to the airstrip and waited for Mendoza to arrive.

Chapter Twenty-nine

Kevin Brannigan stood on the tiny airstrip in Pecos waiting for Mendoza. During the hours he waited, he had exchanged his rental car. Confronted by curious stares, he had asked for a car of a different color and size. Before that he had placed calls to Susan's family, asking them if she had ever mentioned a Texas rancher named John Cressman. From each member of the family the reply had been negative. The remainder of his time had been spent fruitlessly pacing the floor.

When Mendoza walked down the steps from the small plane, Brannigan greeted him with an enthusiasm worthy of a co-conspirator and listening ear. The first and foremost thing they had in common was their love for the Corps. Mendoza loved being a Marine, and he worked hard at it. Brannigan felt more hopeful just having Mendoza with him. He was a good friend to have at any time, but he was a great friend to have in a crunch.

Now, the two of them went straight to Brannigan's motel room and launched their plans with maps spread across the bed. Brannigan drew a sketch of the ranch, or what he had seen of it, and the town and gave Mendoza a full description of the rancher and housekeeper and several of the townspeople.

Mendoza had brought along a Nikon 35 with an ultra zoom and wore inconspicuous clothing—definitely no uniform. The last thing they wanted to do was draw attention to their activities. Mendoza would go in broad daylight—who wanted to cross that terrain in the dark?—and because of that fact he would go alone. Anyone who had seen Brannigan already and knew the rancher could become nervous if Brannigan appeared again.

As Mendoza changed clothes and readied the camera, Brannigan worked up his courage to respond to the look on Mendoza's face. That look had been there when Mendoza deplaned and on the drive to the motel, unspoken but there all the same.

Mendoza got into the car with the maps and sketches beside him, camera and film tucked into a pack along with a few useful tools Brannigan had purchased. Just before he left, Brannigan stopped Mendoza and told him, "I appreciate what you're doing. I couldn't have asked just anybody."

Mendoza said, "Yeah, yeah," but he smiled.

"I want to know what's going on out there. You understand? No matter what you find. I don't want you to pretty it up."

Mendoza studied Brannigan's face. "Sure," he said. He turned the key, started the ignition, and then he was gone. Brannigan went back into the motel room, back to the incessant pacing and the anxiety.

Some time later Mendoza slid into a more comfortable position and lay in the sun exposed only to a few curious buzzards, which he hoped had other prey and didn't have their eyes on him. He glanced overhead at the vastness above him, sheer blue and clear, and thought the area was probably too remote for planes too far off any flight path. He could not believe this place was on the way to anything even remotely civilized. Mendoza looked at his watch. One hour and forty-five minutes since he had moved into position, and he'd seen nothing at all. The worst of it had been the trek from the fence line, miles in the heat carrying equipment on his back. Of course that was nothing new; carrying equipment and traveling by foot over rough terrain he could do—in fact, it was what he did all the time—but snakes were another matter. Fifteen feet onto the property after cutting the fence about a quarter of a mile past the gate, Mendoza had run into a snake. A rattler at that. He would rather dodge flak from an M16A2 than run into a snake. The diamond-shaped pattern on its back had been an unnecessary clue once he'd heard the rattle. One swift thrust of his knife, and the snake was separated from its head. He felt the skin crawl on the back of his neck, just thinking about it. He did not want to hang around this place past dark.

Movement down around the ranch house caught his attention. Someone had come out of the house, followed by another person. Mendoza picked up the binoculars as the first person gesticulated, raising one arm and pointing, and then went back into the house. The second, smaller figure walked toward the pool. Mendoza adjusted the scope on the binoculars and zeroed in on the area of the pool. *Bingo!* The long, shapely legs of Susan Brannigan; Mendoza looked at her, seeing every curve. He'd always noticed how good she looked—there wasn't anything wrong with his vision—but this was his friend's wife. And what was she doing in this outpost of civilization, he wondered.

Brannigan's wife sat beside the pool in a lounge chair, looking for all the world like a guest on vacation. Mendoza pulled the camera from his pack, snapped the lens into place, and focused. He had to get a clear picture to show Brannigan to be certain it was his wife. *He isn't going to like it;* that one thought kept running over and over in Mendoza's head.

He took several shots, then checked the terrain again. Nothing else moved except the cattle in the distance. Another ten or fifteen shots and he stowed his gear in the pack and moved back down the rocky hillside. He was glad to be getting out of this place, and he'd be even happier when he reached the motel, far from anything that slithered on the ground.

When he reached the edge of the property, he pushed the fence into place, hoping it would remain unnoticed, at least for a few days. The car sat where he had left it, just off the road, but the temperature inside had reached over one hundred degrees. Perspiration ran down the sides of his face from his hairline, but he paid little attention. His one worry was Brannigan's reaction to his news.

The motel room door jerked open immediately, and he knew Brannigan had been watching for him, most likely pacing the floor. Mendoza avoided Brannigan's eyes as he passed him to enter the room. Dropping the film off at the local developer had been a good choice too. Mendoza had to tip the guy to drop everything and develop the pictures he'd taken first. The hundred-dollar bill Mendoza had given the guy provided incentive.

"Well?" Brannigan's outward calm was in direct contrast to the expression in his eyes.

"You were right," Mendoza told him. "She's there."

Faced with the truth, Brannigan didn't know what to think or feel. "You saw her? You're sure? There's no chance you're mistaken?"

"I saw her."

"No chance it could be someone else?"

"No. And I got pictures. I took half a roll to make sure. Some of the shots should be clear enough to prove it."

"You took pictures of her? She was outside? What was she doing? Who was she with?"

"She wasn't with anyone. Someone came out of the house ahead of her, but he went back in."

"He?"

"Yeah. I think it was your rancher." Mendoza hated to say more.

"What did she do then?"

"Nothing. She just sat down. Alone." As he said it, Mendoza sat down in the one chair in the motel room that was meant for comfort but wasn't all that comfortable. He was content to be inside and cooling off in his sweat-stained shirt.

Brannigan's brow furrowed. "She sat down? Outside? In this heat?"

"By the pool."

"By the pool?" Brannigan felt as if he had lost his ability to reason. His wife disappears, and he's frantic with worry, but when he finds her, she's sitting by a swimming pool? "She was sitting by the pool? In a swimsuit?"

"Yes." Mendoza cringed inwardly, waiting for the explosion. Who was it in history that had killed the messenger for bringing bad news?

Brannigan turned away, and Mendoza could only guess what he was feeling. He watched as Brannigan paced across the room and back. Brannigan stopped. "What about the children?" Brannigan asked, his voice strained.

"I didn't see a sign of them, but they must be there. She wouldn't be there without them. You know that."

"Do I?" Brannigan said. He pushed his fingers through his hair. "Do I? I don't know anything anymore." He asked, "Can I be sure of anything?"

Brannigan's face looked tortured. Mendoza had seen him in bad situations before—even in combat his face had remained calm and in control. Mendoza had never seen him like this. He told Brannigan, "You can be sure your children are safe and with their mother." And then he added, "You can be sure she wouldn't let anything happen to them."

"But why is she there? And where did she meet up with that jerk cowhand? And what is he to her?" He said these things quietly enough. No shouting, no elaborate gestures of outrage, but to one who'd known him a long time, Mendoza knew that the rage was held in check at great effort. Brannigan contained it under the surface; the explosion was still to come.

The restless energy in the room infected Mendoza, and he got up and went to the window and looked out. He wondered what his own wife was doing right now. Was she preparing dinner? He wished he were with her.

Brannigan crossed the room and pulled a bottle of Scotch from his bag. He opened it and put the bottle to his mouth, but he stopped. He thought better of it and put the bottle down. There were no easy answers.

"Where's the film?" he asked Mendoza.

"What?" Mendoza's thoughts had drifted.

"Where is the film? The pictures you took." Brannigan faced Mendoza. "Where's your proof?"

"I took the film to be developed."

"In this place? That could take days!"

"That's true; they don't have one-hour film-developing here, or at least not in the place I took it. But the pictures will be ready in less than an hour. I got the guy to put them ahead of everything else he had. You owe me a hundred, by the way."

Brannigan laughed, but it was a hollow echo; there was nothing humorous in the situation. "They'd better be good," he said. "I'll need them. For proof."

Mendoza didn't follow. "Proof?"

"If I'm caught breaking into the ranch." He didn't explain. He didn't have to. The truth had brought with it pain, and that pain overrode everything else. It poured into the room, into the very air in the place, and it suffocated him. He looked at the bottle of Scotch again and fingered it.

Mendoza told him, "That won't help."

Brannigan knew it. He put the bottle away, out of sight. "I hate it when you're right."

Mendoza laughed. "Good thing it doesn't happen often, then."

Brannigan's noncommittal, "Humph," preceded his sudden slump into the chair Mendoza had occupied earlier.

They fell silent for a while until Mendoza told him, "The votes aren't all in."

Brannigan looked at him. "What's that supposed to mean?"

Mendoza pulled a straight-backed chair up to face Brannigan. "I'm just saying that all we know for sure is that she's there. And that's good news. You know where she is."

"Yeah, but—"

"*But* you don't know *why* she's there. She didn't come here to see him. She was on her way to her sister's—a legitimate move for her to make while you were gone. A trip, right? A short vacation to see family." Mendoza counted off on his fingers. "You know she had car trouble, right?"

"Right." Brannigan had seen the proof of that with his own eyes when he'd broken into the garage.

"You also know that she loves you and that, so far as you know, she never even knew this guy before two weeks ago, right?"

Brannigan stared at him with a level gaze. "So what are you saying?"

"I'm saying that the one thing you don't know is why she's there, and you don't need to be thinking it's over when it isn't. The rancher told you he'd never seen her. Now we *know* he's lying, and that means one of two things. Either he's lying 'cause she doesn't want you to know she's there, or he's lying because *he* doesn't want you to know she's there." Mendoza stopped. "Either way it doesn't mean they're—" Mendoza stopped again. He only had so much nerve after all.

"Say it." Brannigan told him.

"It doesn't mean they're involved."

Brannigan thought about it carefully, and his friend's logical sequence of thoughts brought a small measure of reassurance.

"Besides," Mendoza added, "you don't really think she'd go for him, do you? A tired old cowpoke when she has a Marine?" Mendoza's comment elicited the response he'd sought.

Brannigan laughed—actually, it was more like a snort. "He'd never go off on missions; he'd be home all the time."

"Yeah, there's that. But, you know, I have this theory that the gals really like that, although they won't admit it. I mean, think of all the fun you two have when you get back from being gone."

Brannigan didn't react to that one, but he'd started thinking. He had enough ego to acknowledge he was what Susan wanted, and she'd never liked the cowboy type, not even if he was a real rancher. At any rate, Brannigan would not give up. He stood up abruptly. "Let's go get those pictures." They started for the door, and Brannigan added, "And, by the way, I hate it when you tick points off on your fingers like that. It's so methodical, so anal."

Mendoza laughed as they headed out the door. Neither of them even thought about going to the police, even though they now knew for certain that Susan was at the ranch.

Chapter Thirty

The end to each day meant a lessening of the heat. It also meant more of Cressman's company than Susan had to tolerate during the day. Cressman told Maria to feed the children at the usual dinner hour, then told Susan to shower and change into something nice for dinner. Filled with an apathetic lethargy, Susan went to do as Cressman had ordered. She showered and dressed, but then she spent an hour reading bedtime stories and holding the children. By the time they fell asleep, she had strengthened her resolve. She watched her children sleeping. This was the night. Somehow she was going to escape with both children. On a horse. What was that old song about a horse with no name? It didn't matter. She didn't care about anything as long as she got her children away from the place safely.

Cressman, in the end, had to come and get her. He took her out to the patio, where Maria had arranged dinner near the pool. She had prepared *enchiladas verdes*, and Susan discovered that, in spite of everything, she was hungry.

"You're looking beautiful tonight," John told her. "The blue in your dress is exactly the color of your eyes."

Susan made no comment as she dug into her salad. She had nothing to say to him.

"I had hoped you'd be more comfortable here by now." He watched her with an intensity that disturbed her. He had put on a dress shirt and black pants, something other than the usual jeans and work shirt.

165

"I will never be comfortable here," she stated as matter-of-factly as she could.

"Now, why do you say that? Haven't I done everything I could to make you feel at home?" He looked disturbed.

"But this isn't my home. I won't ever be happy here. You can't make me." In spite of the fact that she sounded like an angry and whiny child, she felt good about saying it.

"I was afraid you felt that way." He was quiet for a few minutes, watching her. Suddenly he got up and came around the table toward her. He ran his hands across her shoulders and caressed them slowly. "I think I've given you too much time to adjust. Maybe what you needed all along was more time with me to make your adjustment."

Susan gripped the arms of her chair. "What are you talking about? What do you mean?"

"You know what I mean, Susan. You're a beautiful woman, and I've been thinking about you. About very little else, in fact." He pulled her off the chair and held her.

"Don't." She turned her face away.

"It's for the best," he assured her. "Believe me, it made all the difference with Ellen." At that he kissed her, and his fingers gripped her arms, and the pressure of his mouth forced her head back. Susan pulled away, but he reacted by tightening his grip, and she nearly fell. He grabbed her, stopping her fall. "I just want you to be happy here, Susan." A soft voice spoke in Spanish beside them. Cressman released her so abruptly that Susan fell back into the chair. Maria stood beside them, avoiding Susan's eyes, and spoke quietly to John.

He relayed the message to Susan. "The boy is sick."

"What?" Susan jumped up. "What happened?"

"She says he threw up."

Susan ran into the house and down the hall to the room that the children slept in. Bryan lay awake in the middle of the bed; he looked pale and frightened. He reached for her as soon as he saw her. "Mommy? I couldn't find you."

"I was outside, buddy. Are you feeling sick?" She held him

close on the bed, then transferred to the rocking chair and sat holding him, rocking gently. She was not certain who clung to whom, but it was a comfort to both of them. Bryan was sick again during the night, but he settled into a peaceful slumber after one o'clock. John came to the door several times to check on them, but he went away without a word. Susan stayed with Bryan all night and finally closed her eyes when the morning light slipped into the room.

The photos were clear. Susan's long legs stretched out on a chaise. In the picture her hair was a blond glow in the sunlight. Brannigan leaned against the car and stared at the photographs. His wife looked like a woman on vacation, possibly trying to get a tan.

After a close look at the pictures, Mendoza pulled one out, inspecting it so closely that his nose almost touched the glossy print. He turned abruptly and went into the now-closed store where the film processing had been done. The hundred-dollar bill had done the trick, keeping the store open past closing. Brannigan sat in the car while he looked at the pictures, one agonizing shot after another, and each one a death knell for his hope of getting back what he once had. The heat inside the car had driven him out to where he stood beside the front fender. Though he'd felt a blow to the pit of his stomach when he saw the pictures, he couldn't deny that it was definitely Susan. She appeared so relaxed; he felt sick. After fifteen minutes Mendoza returned. Brannigan wondered what he was up to and why he'd gone back into the store. What to do next was the chief occupation of Brannigan's mind.

Mendoza carried a large paper in his hand. "Take a look at this," he said. He pulled the paper forward and explained, "I had the guy blow up one of the shots because I thought I saw something." He held the print out to Brannigan.

Brannigan took it, looked at it, and wondered what it was Mendoza wanted him to see. "Look at her face," Mendoza told him.

Brannigan stared at the picture; he looked more closely, and he reacted, just as Mendoza expected. Brannigan gasped. He saw something on Susan's face, on the curve of her cheekbone, and it was that that had made him suck in his breath. They were tears. Brannigan looked at Mendoza and then at the picture again. Susan was crying. What did it mean? Mendoza summed it up in few words. "I don't know whose idea it was for her to be there, but life is not what it appears down on the old ranch."

Brannigan looked at Mendoza, and suddenly they were both grinning. Susan's unhappiness was the first positive sign they'd seen. They thought it over carefully for the next half hour, and the solution, when it occurred to them, would be different than what anyone might expect. The biggest challenge lay in obtaining the gear needed to penetrate the ranch. Pecos, Texas, had nothing they needed but, possibly, a couple of hunting rifles. Mendoza remembered he had a buddy stationed at Fort Bliss in El Paso. The two of them had grown up in the same neighborhood, but, to Mendoza's dismay, his buddy had joined the Army and not the Marines. Mendoza's wife and Raul's wife were cousins, so they kept in touch.

Mendoza drove to El Paso and back within hours. He said he had engaged in a little noncom wheeling and dealing. Brannigan never learned the details of the arrangement, and Mendoza assured him that he was better off not knowing. At any rate Mendoza returned with two NODS, the night-vision devices used by the Army, along with other items he thought he and Brannigan would need. By the afternoon of the following day they felt ready for anything.

Brannigan exchanged the rental car a third time to get one that had never been seen in the area. This time, to stall arguments over yet another exchange, he explained he'd need one that he could drive out of the state. He also arranged for a car for Mendoza to use to return the gear to Fort Bliss and a return flight home from there. The trip had become damaging to his cash flow and his credit cards as well. If it paid off, he didn't care. He wanted his wife back, and any cost would be worth it. If not—well, he didn't even want to think about that. He couldn't go there.

Bryan's stomach had settled, but his small face still looked pale. By afternoon he had resumed his normal pace. He felt so much better that Susan let him play in the shallow end of the pool while Chrissy napped inside the house.

Bryan paddled like a puppy, splashing his mother and laughing uproariously each time he succeeded. Susan held her arms stretched toward him, trying to get him to come out.

"I can swim like Daddy," he said.

"Yes, you can," she answered thoughtfully. "Do you miss Daddy?"

"Daddy will come. Daddy will come get us."

"He will?" Susan hadn't the heart to tell him that his daddy didn't even know where they were.

Bryan splashed around and slapped one palm against the water's surface; he enjoyed the feel of the splat and the effect it made. He said, "He'll get baby Chrissy too. Can we take Albert home with us?"

"Albert?" He had named the calf Albert. "I don't think we can keep a calf at our house."

"He isn't big."

"But he will get very big."

"How big?" Bryan wanted to know.

Susan put her hands out, far apart.

"I want to take Albert home with me," Bryan whined.

Susan tried to reason with him, but nothing worked. She thought about Kevin's way of reasoning with Bryan. He'd always been patient and talked to him in a calm tone. When Kevin was home, he listened to the children. He loved to read stories to them, and he played with them. Now that he was nowhere around, now that she'd lost him, she remembered so many of the things he had done and all the good times they'd had. When they'd been outside for forty-five minutes, she realized that was enough time in the sun, and she told Bryan, "Time to go in, buddy." She had to pull Bryan from the pool and dry him off. He resisted, and he was still fussing when she carried him into the house.

Once inside, Susan heated up the homemade chicken noodle soup that Maria had made and fed it to Bryan. She kept busy, but her thoughts centered on Kevin. She could picture his tall, lean body and his dark hair. His hair had a stubborn streak and would turn in a slight wave if it was grown out. The symmetry of his face and his strong nose gave him a look of strength that she thought was sometimes deceiving. Oh, he was strong physically, and he could handle a command, but every once in a while, in a rare moment, she glimpsed a need to connect, a need that only she could fill. The need was not sexual but intimate, an intimacy that included the children and their lives together, their connection as a family apart from the rest of the world, contained in their own little core group. In earlier days they would have shared the same cave, wickiup, thatched cottage, or whatever. Kevin had a sense of that connection that pervaded his deeper being; why hadn't she realized that before? In his career he could lead men into training, into battle if it became necessary, but when the adrenaline rush died, when duty was done, he needed to reconnect with a primordial reason for life. The work he did excited him, but even in his thirties he knew that he needed something more than a career. And what would he have if he hadn't developed his family bond? She realized in a moment of clarity that he knew this and that was why he wanted to hold on tight when he was home with them. Why hadn't she understood all this before? Had she discovered it too late?

No. She refused to believe that.

Susan had formulated plans already and would have made her escape the night before if Bryan hadn't been sick. Before she thought about the horse, Susan had searched everywhere for the keys to one of the trucks or the Cadillac. It would be so much easier and more comfortable to get away in a car or truck, the kind of transportation she was used to. She felt sure Cressman would slip up and leave them lying about if she waited long enough. Taking his Cadillac would have added a further, almost perverse pleasure over and above escaping. But she'd never seen so much as one key lying around. She could not escape on foot carrying both children. That much she knew for certain. She could walk out on her own, but there was no way she would leave the two of them, not even temporarily. Not only would it frighten Bryan and upset Chrissy's feeding schedule, but she feared what Cressman might do if he became angry at her.

Susan remained in the nursery long after the baby fell asleep and Bryan finally nodded off. Cressman came to the door and told her he was waiting to have dinner with her, but she feigned illness, telling him that she thought she was coming down with the same stomach problem that had plagued Bryan. Her story was unconvincing even to her own ears, but Cressman bought it and left her alone.

Once he was gone, she went to bed, but she couldn't sleep; she was consumed with worry. Could she get the saddle onto the horse properly? And could she keep the horse, not to mention the kids, from making a sound? And, most important of all, could she control the horse? The last thing she wanted was to place the children into greater danger. The lack of sleep the night before caught up with her, and she found it increasingly difficult to keep her eyes open as she waited until the house grew quiet and she could be certain that Cressman was sound asleep.

Chapter Thirty-one

Night dropped over the land and enveloped them like a black cloth, leaving nothing but tiny stars that looked the millions of distant miles away that they were in reality. The car moved through the small town as silently as only a new vehicle could. When they reached the ranch gate, they continued on another three-quarters of a mile down the road before parking the car. Leaving it well off the side of the road, the two of them trekked back across the terrain, cut through the fence, and slipped in between the now-ineffective wire inside the perimeter of the ranch.

Mendoza cautioned Brannigan about snakes, but Brannigan's thoughts were on two-legged varmints and the ordeal ahead. What would the culmination of this night bring? Could he deal with the outcome, no matter what it was? He knew he had to face whatever it was. Clouds parted, and the moon appeared, but it was a mere sliver. The glow it cast was soft, not enough to see well. They followed the road and kept several feet off to the side, making the route less direct but easier than crossing the country. Brannigan resisted the urge to use the NODs, since there was enough light to outline the drive and any large, darker obstacles. If they'd driven in part of the way, they could have covered the distance more quickly, but they believed their best bet would be the element of surprise. The distance to the house took half an hour, but they reached it and maintained a deadly quiet while keeping an alert eye out for movement. Not a thing moved anywhere around them.

The two of them inched toward the house with no sound between them. Their training hadn't deserted them. Together they skirted a corner of the house to a door at one end. A mop hung on a hook beside the door; a trash can stood nearby. The door led to the back entrance nearest the kitchen, the room least likely to be occupied in the middle of the night.

Brannigan silently slit the screen, and Mendoza pulled a plastic strip from his pocket to manipulate the lock, but the door opened easily at the turn of the knob. No concerns about burglars this far into the country and away from everything.

The Night Optical Devices cast a greenish glow to all the objects in sight. The kitchen was large and spotless, but it appeared as an alien land tinged in green as they moved through it. Brannigan entered the dining room with Mendoza inches behind him, oddly ill at ease without the familiar M16A2s in their hands, though both of them hoped there would be no reason to need them. The recon Marine's mission was to get in, accomplish the reconnaissance, and then get out, and that was their intention here. The room contained a large table and chairs and nothing else of interest. They crossed it and slipped into the hall. Now the situation became more complicated. The hall led to the living room, but there were several other doors that opened off the hall. Which to choose was the immediate problem. Brannigan made an educated guess about the master bedroom. His plan was to systematically check all the others.

The first door opened quietly, but it was a bathroom. He closed that one and moved to the next on the left. An empty bedroom. He shut the door and moved across the hall to the next door on the right.

Opening the door, he looked into a bedroom. The bed occupied the greater portion of the room, and, in the middle of the bed, Susan lay sleeping. Brannigan didn't move for a minute, overcome by the sight of his wife after so long. There had been times when he'd doubted he would ever find her, that he would ever see her again. Or his children.

The dim glow from the window turned her hair to silver, but the NODs gave it a silver-green cast. Her sleeping posture, the touch of eyelashes on cheekbone, lent an ethereal quality to the scene. Was it really Susan? He moved to the side of the bed. He wanted to touch her, to look at her face, her body, to feel her arms around him. She lay facing in the other direction. How could he wake her without scaring her half to death? Mendoza watched, waiting for Brannigan's lead. After a brief hesitation, Brannigan reached out quickly and enclosed her mouth with one hand. She woke instantly and began to struggle. He climbed onto the bed and pulled her against him hard. Susan fought to get free of him. She struggled and tried to kick him. He stood in the center of the bed and pulled her to her feet and heard her teeth grind as she fought his hold on her. Her teeth sank into his hand. He said in a loud whisper, "Susan. Susan. Baby, it's me!"

She stopped her struggle instantly and tried to turn her head to see his face. Brannigan pulled the NOD off his head. "It's me," he whispered.

She twisted her body to face him when he released his hold on her mouth. "Kevin?"

"Yes."

"Oh, Kevin." She threw her arms around him and buried her face against his neck. She clung to him, afraid he was a figment of her desperation and her overwhelming desire to escape.

Brannigan stepped down off the bed and pulled Susan with him. She raised her face to him and kissed him with all the pent-up frustration she'd felt for weeks; then she again buried her face against his neck. Brannigan looked at Mendoza, barely visible to him in the dark room.

Mendoza grinned. "I guess that answers one question."

Brannigan smiled. He held Susan with one arm and whispered, "Where are the kids?"

Reality returned with a heavy thud. "They're in there," she

told him. "But we have to be careful. He might hear us. He might—"

The door burst open, and Brannigan stared down the barrel of a shotgun. Cressman came into the room and demanded, "Get back, both of you!"

The three of them stood as still as statues and stared, caught like guilty thieves in the night. "Get over here, Susan," Cressman barked.

"No," Brannigan argued. "It's over. She's coming with me."

Cressman's eyes narrowed. "She's not going anywhere. And you," he yelled at Mendoza, "get over there." Mendoza inched back to where he'd been standing before the door opened.

"You ever seen what buckshot can do to a face?"

"You aren't going to shoot," Brannigan said.

His voice sounded calm, but Susan knew him better than that. He was shaking with uncontrollable fury.

"You want to take that chance? It's not going to be your face I shoot."

Brannigan blanched, and both he and Mendoza looked at Susan. She looked terrified, and why wouldn't she be? The man was unhinged. And dangerous.

Susan let go of Kevin's arm and took a step toward Cressman. She'd known it wasn't going to be that easy to get away.

Kevin said, "No!" and reached for her.

Cressman snapped the shotgun around and rammed the butt into Brannigan's pretty-boy looks with a satisfying crack. Susan cried out, and Mendoza jumped toward Cressman.

"Get over here!" Cressman shouted, and he yanked Susan against him. He backed into the hall, taking her with him.

Brannigan followed.

"Stay back!" Cressman ordered, but Brannigan came on.

Mendoza lunged for the rancher but he tripped and hit his head against the door frame as he went down. Susan banged the small table against the wall as Cressman pulled her into the dining room. He was heading for the back door, but what was he thinking? Where could he go?

She watched Kevin's face; blood glistened on his lip. His eyes never left Cressman's face.

But Cressman altered his direction slightly to get past the dining room table, and Brannigan lunged. He knocked Susan to the floor and went for Cressman's throat. They crashed to the floor, taking chairs with them. Brannigan held the rancher down, and all of his past anguish flooded through him. He wanted to bash his face in for what he'd put them through. He'd never felt such rage in his life, and he slammed his fist into Cressman's jaw. But Cressman was no weakling in spite of his additional twenty years. He gouged Kevin's face and pushed hard, gaining the upper hand, flipping Brannigan onto his back.

Susan pulled herself up and tried to get a hold on Cressman, grasping only his shirt. The two men rolled and knocked her back onto the floor, onto her backside, and her head cracked against a table leg.

Cressman rose to his feet, but Brannigan grabbed him around the waist. Cressman kneed Brannigan in the chest, knocking him back, but he pulled the rancher down with him. Cressman slammed into the younger man, knocking the breath out of him. Brannigan gasped, paralyzed for a moment, and Cressman jerked back to his feet and reached for Susan, dragging her upright. Her hair was matted with blood.

Brannigan kicked Cressman in the calf muscle, and the rancher went down. He released his hold on Susan, and she fell onto the floor again. She cried out from the pain, and Brannigan thrust himself onto the rancher, gripping his shoulders, his thumbs pressing into the flesh above his collarbone down deep toward his throat. Their eyes locked together, sweat covered their faces, and grunts emitted through gritted teeth.

Mendoza staggered into the room and saw Susan on the floor. He pulled her up and handed her into the one remaining upright chair with care.

Legs flailed in the gut-wrenching struggle on the floor. Kevin fought to get on top; Cressman pushed him off and over, throwing Brannigan into Mendoza. Mendoza's legs buckled, and he went down backward with Brannigan on top of him.

Cressman got to his feet and disappeared out the door. Brannigan pulled himself up and helped Mendoza to his feet, and then he reached for Susan. "Are you all right?"

She nodded. "I think so."

"You?" he asked Mendoza.

"Yeah." Mendoza laughed. "I'm in one piece."

"Come on." Brannigan kissed Susan. "Let's go get the kids and get out of here."

Chapter Thirty-two

They crossed the hall into the bedroom where they'd found Susan and then on into the next room. Brannigan went to the crib first and picked up his sleeping daughter. He held her close for a second; her warmth and baby scent touched him and filled him with emotion, leaving a lump in his throat. The baby slept through the exchange as he held her out to Susan.

When they turned toward the youth bed, they found it empty. Mendoza flicked a penlight on.

"Where's Bryan?" Susan demanded, her words spoken low but piercing the night as much as if she had shouted them.

On the cot, Maria had pulled herself to a sitting position, but she held the sheet up to her chin. Her eyes were wide with fright.

"Where's the boy?" Brannigan demanded.

Maria stared at the three of them.

"She doesn't speak English," Susan told them.

Mendoza moved toward the bed. *"Donde esta el niño?"*

Maria looked up at him, clearly terrified. Mendoza softened his tone. *"Señora, por favor, diga me. Donde esta el niño?"*

Maria pointed toward the door to the hall. The door stood open.

At the far end of the house, a door slammed.

"He's got him, Kevin. He's taken Bryan."

After everything else, it was finally too much, the last straw, the final indignity. Susan's anger burst into pure, unadulterated

178

rage. "He's not going to take him!" Susan bolted out the door, still carrying Chrissy.

Brannigan and Mendoza ran after her and reached the kitchen as she disappeared out the back door shouting, "That's enough!" she shouted. "No more!"

Cressman was visible in the pale moonlight as he headed for the barn, carrying Bryan in his arms. Bryan looked back over Cressman's shoulder. "Mommy!" he cried. "Mommy!"

"John!" she screamed. "John! Stop! You give him back to me!"

But Cressman ignored her and disappeared into the barn with Bryan on his shoulder. Susan ran with Chrissy bobbing up and down in her arms. She reached the barn and stood surrounded by total, absolute silence. Cressman had disappeared and, with him, Bryan.

Brannigan and Mendoza rushed in and found her standing in the middle of the barn, looking around. "What the—? Where is he?" Brannigan asked.

"I don't know," Susan said, fighting tears.

They listened. Nothing stirred. The hush was so complete, they could hear crickets chirping outside. The mare shifted her weight; the puppies squeaked, searching for their mother and nuzzling. They realized then that the barn was far from quiet, but it was devoid of human sounds.

The mama dog climbed out of her box and began to bark loudly at the intruders; she pitched a fit, her fur standing on end. Mendoza and Brannigan eyed the dog warily.

"She has puppies," Susan warned them.

The dog continued to bark, the sound sharp and loud within the walls of the barn. Mendoza and Brannigan backed a few feet away, hoping to appease the dog. Any other time, the sight of the two Marines backing away from a dog protecting her pups might have made Susan laugh, but there was nothing remotely humorous in this situation. Deciding she had warned them sufficiently, the dog moved back into the stall, into the box where her puppies waited. Mendoza moved outside the barn to search, and Brannigan checked through the stalls and every corner of the barn systematically.

Mendoza returned. "No sign of him anywhere."

"Listen!" Susan said. "I heard something." She whispered, "Up there," and she pointed toward the hayloft.

Kevin started up the ladder; the wood creaked.

"Don't come up here!" Cressman's voice came from above their heads, but neither he nor Bryan was visible. Kevin climbed higher, and the old ladder announced each step.

"Get away!" Cressman called out. "I have a lighter! I'll make this hay go up in flames!"

Kevin stopped. The loft hung above his head by several feet. Could it be a bluff? Did the man have a lighter with him? And, more important, would he use it? Brannigan hesitated, then lifted his foot to the next rung.

Susan watched Kevin's foot inch up in slow motion, and she yelled out, "John? John, listen to me. Don't do this! You don't want to do this. Give Bryan to me. Please."

"Get them out of here!" Cressman's voice, ragged with emotion, fell around them, but only Susan reacted. She looked at the two men, but before she could even suggest it, Kevin warned, "I'm not leaving you alone here."

"Get them out of here!" Cressman yelled again.

Kevin's face was set; he would be inflexible. Susan pleaded, "Just go over by the door. Both of you." When they made no move to go, she said, "He'll do it. He means it. You have to go. Please."

Kevin started down the ladder. As the wood strained, Susan yelled, "He's getting down, John! They're leaving."

She watched Kevin back down the ladder, and he came close to relieve her of the baby. "You aren't going up there," he said. It was not a demand but a statement. She watched the two men move to the door and not one step farther.

"They're gone now, John. Give Bryan to me."

"They haven't gone."

"John, please. You don't want to do this. Give me my baby. You know what it's like to lose a son."

"Why couldn't you be happy here?" John's anguish ripped out of the very depths of his soul, and it wrenched her even though she'd never suspected that she could feel any sympathy for him.

"I wanted to give you everything. Everything."

"Come on down, John, and let's talk it over."

"There's no use. You're with him now. You chose him. He won't make you happy. He won't ever appreciate you and love you the way I do. He can't give you what I can, but you chose him."

Susan looked toward the door, at Kevin's face, the expression in his eyes. He watched her. If she made even the slightest move toward the ladder, he was prepared to stop her.

Mendoza took the baby and went into the house to call the sheriff and the state police and anyone else he could get a rise out of in this isolated and lonely place.

A scuffle ensued in the hayloft and drew Susan's eyes upward. She heard whimpers, then Bryan's voice. "I want my mommy. Mommy! Mommy!"

"Mommy's here, Bryan. John, you're scaring him. Please give him to me."

"You could have had it all." John's voice came across in a tone that was inconsolable. "You should have been happy here. But you want to leave, just like she did."

"I'm coming up, John. I'm coming up to get Bryan."

Kevin started toward her, but she held a hand out to stop him. She put a finger over her lips, warning him to say nothing. She climbed onto the ladder, then moved to the second rung. Her hand, held palm out toward Kevin, issued warning, and he remained where he was, but the effort was obvious; he was barely restrained. She stepped onto the third rung and then the fourth, and Kevin's expression intensified.

"John," she called out again. "Come on, John. Give Bryan to

me. Please, if you care about me at all, don't do it. Don't make me go through the hell you went through. I couldn't bear it." Her voice broke; tears clouded her vision and rolled down her face. "Please, John."

The hayloft was enveloped in an ominous silence. Even Bryan's whimpers had stopped. The mare stamped her feet, but nothing stirred above. Susan opened her mouth to speak, but the sound of rustling in the hay stopped her. Movement above her head held her motionless; hay fluttered to the ground. Bryan's legs appeared from the loft, dangling above her head. Only John's arms were visible as he lowered Bryan from the edge of the loft. Susan leaned her body weight against the ladder and reached for her son, enclosing his little body within her arms. She shifted him to one arm and grasped the ladder with the other before she started down. Kevin stood at the bottom of the ladder and pulled both of them into his arms. She leaned her head against him, sinking into the security of his strength. She had everything she wanted now; she had her family back, and everyone was intact. For a moment all else faded into insignificance. Nothing else mattered.

And then, remembering Cressman, Susan pulled out of her cocoon and called to him. "Come on down now, John. Let's talk."

Silence was her only answer, and then an ominous click above their heads followed by a loud *whump,* and the dry hay burst into flames. At the bottom of the ladder they stood immobilized by shock. The smell of smoke trickled down into Susan's lungs, and her stomach churned with nausea. The fire came back to her—all of it. The smoke, the flames burning up the wall across the hall, her cheek pressed into the wood of the closet floor. She stared in stunned silence.

Chapter Thirty-three

The hay burned with a speed and ferocity that startled them, long fingers of flames licking upward. The barn burst into life with the sounds of frightened animals: the whinny of horses, hooves stamped in frightened agitation, the dog barking and the cow bellowing, her big eyes wide with fear. The animals were agitated and fearful, and with good reason, because the fire had become a living threat, consuming the loft and everything above them.

Brannigan tried to reach Cressman, but the entire loft was aflame. He pulled Susan and Bryan out of the barn and then returned to release the horses from the stalls. He didn't have to force the horses out of the barn; once he opened the gates to the stalls, they ran out into the night. Mendoza returned, thrust little Chrissy at Susan, and began to help. He carried the calf to safety because, frozen with fear, it would not move on its own. When he walked out with the calf, the cow followed.

Ranch hands ran up and pulled water hoses from several spigots around the yard, but it was too little and too late. Maria brought buckets from the house, and they carried water from the pool. Even that was not enough to stop the flames. They could not get enough water fast enough. The fire rose in peaks toward the roof of the barn and spread outward toward the walls. Brannigan, Mendoza, and Crabb, the ranch foreman led three more horses from the now half-consumed barn.

Outside, Bryan cried, "The puppies, Mommy! Where are the puppies?"

Susan caught Kevin's arm as he came out with the mare. She reminded him about the dog and her puppies, and then she moved the children farther back to a safe distance. She would not go back into that house, but she reached a glider on the lawn and sat down facing the black night instead of the flames that were lighting up the sky behind her.

Both of the children clung to her; even Chrissy at such a young age sensed the tension around her. Susan held them so tightly, they laid their heads against her, finding comfort in the echo of her steady heartbeat. Before long the three of them were breathing together, the deep even breath of near sleep. As difficult as it was, Susan would not look at the scene behind them, and she tried her best to block out the noise and the acrid smell of the fire. Chrissy fell asleep first, but even Bryan succumbed and finally fell asleep against her. She was their rock and their stability, and that was all she cared about.

The county sheriff and his deputy arrived, the sheriff questioning everyone at the scene while the deputy tried to gather evidence. When the state police arrived, jurisdiction became an issue, but the two law-enforcement agencies cooperated and worked together. The deputy and two state troopers sifted through the burned rubble, searching for remains.

All the animals had been saved, but the barn was a total loss; it had burned to the ground, taking John Cressman with it. Susan gave her statement to the sheriff, and she learned, for the first time, that John had told his ranch hands and Maria that she was his niece who was staying at the ranch while she was getting over a difficult divorce. Whether any of them believed it or suspected anything else, none of them said, and they never volunteered more than that.

Brannigan and Mendoza were as shocked as the law-enforcement officers to learn how Susan had been drugged and taken to the ranch. Because of her abduction, the sheriff overlooked Brannigan and Mendoza's illegal entry to the ranch and the house itself. Although she was exhausted, Susan refused to go into the house, but her husband was allowed in to pack their few belongings and take them from what was now labeled a crime scene. Mendoza, able to communicate with the ranch hands in Spanish, got one of them to drive him out to the road where he and Brannigan had left the rental car.

When he pulled up with the car, Susan climbed into the front seat. She held both children and would not relinquish them, not even to get a little more comfortable. Bryan woke as they got into the car. He looked up at Susan with drowsy eyes before settling his weight against her again. The heat from their small bodies comforted her.

Susan looked out at the ranch house and the open land beyond as morning arrived and the first light of day began to filter into the night and illuminate the sky. Would life ever be normal again?

Kevin appeared at the window. He leaned his head in and gave her a long, searching look, and then he pressed his face against her cheek. He smelled of smoke and burned wood, and, more than that, of skin, his own individual scent, the individual who'd shared years with her. She turned her face toward him, and, lips lightly parted, she kissed him. He responded in kind, and she wanted to sob with joy. They had very nearly lost each other and all that they had, but it would be all right. They had each other, and they had their children. And they had experienced what it would have meant to lose each other.

Chrissy woke, wet and hungry, and started to cry. Bryan woke up too and said, "I'm hungry."

Susan and Kevin looked at the two children, at Chrissy's face as she cried and Bryan's as he complained, "I want Cheerios, Mommy. I want Cheerios now." Susan and Kevin looked at each other; they were pretty beaten up, but they laughed.

"Business as usual," Kevin told her.

Life was noisy and sometimes even difficult, but it was well on the way to being normal again. Kevin reached into the window, deposited a fat brown puppy into Bryan's lap, and said, "Let's go home."